THE SMUGGLER'S SECRET

ARABELLA LARKSPUR

CHAPTER 1

*K*atherine hesitated, her hands on either side of the train door, feeling almost as though her feet didn't want to move—didn't want to take that final step out onto the platform, but she could feel people behind her and knew there was no turning back.

Moving her hands from the doorway and down by her sides, she grasped the hands of her son and daughter and finally stepped down.

It was so much busier than she was used to. There were people everywhere, smoke and steam from the trains that had come through the station, and the smell of unwashed bodies. If she breathed in too deeply, it felt as though her throat was coated with something unpleasant. She was so far from the clean, salt-tinged air she was used to in Ireland.

She had lived in a town there—busy for the area, but it felt like a small village compared to where she found herself now. She closed her eyes for a moment, trying to gather herself. Everything was new, frightening—but it didn't compare to the fear that had caused her to leave her home.

The home she had always known. The home she had imagined her children would grow up in.

But in the end, she'd had no choice. And as soon as she realised that her and her children's safety relied on leaving everything she'd known, she put things in place as quickly as she could. There were few who knew where she was now, and even fewer who knew why.

Those she'd told would know by now, of course —but she hoped that her sudden disappearance might mean she would soon be forgotten.

A shudder ran through her body, and before she could open her eyes and begin the walk towards the exit of the train station, she could already feel the bustle of people around her. Two people bumped into her—no apologies given. Even so, she couldn't help but murmur a small "sorry" each time it happened.

She looked down at Nora and Liam, seeing the mixture of fear and wonder on their faces. She gave each of their hands a gentle squeeze, trying to reassure them, and then started towards the exit. She hoped she looked more confident than she felt.

Each of them had a small bag slung over their shoulders. There hadn't been time to pack much, and not knowing exactly where she was going had made it difficult to know what to bring. A few changes of clothes for each of them—and barely much more than that.

Amongst Katherine's clothing was a small purse with all the money she had in the world—everything she'd saved from the small jobs she'd done over the years. She knew it wouldn't last long.

First of all, though, she needed to find somewhere for them to stay—lodgings of some kind. Once she'd done that, she would need to look for work.

Everything she did from now on would be to provide for, and protect, her children.

Liam wiggled the hand that was in hers.

"Mum," he said.

She realised she'd been gripping it more tightly than she'd known.

"Sorry," she said softly, loosening her grip and rubbing her thumb carefully over his knuckles.

As they stepped out onto the street, the crowd seemed to thin, though there were still people everywhere she looked—carts and horses, stalls along the roadside. So much to take in, but she kept her head down and walked further away from the train station.

Nancy, a friend from back home who had come to England once before, had given her a vague idea of where the lodging houses might be.

"Not right next to the station," she'd said, "but not too far either. The people travelling into the city—they'll need somewhere to stay. They're just the sort the lodging houses are after."

A few streets away from the station, Katherine began to see signs advertising places to stay.

None of them looked particularly well kept. After passing a few—hoping to find something better—she realised she had no choice.

She would go into the next one she came across and try to secure a place for them, at least for tonight.

After a good night's sleep, she told herself, *surely things will look better.*

. . .

WHEN SHE CAME to the next lodging house, she told herself it looked better than the others she'd passed —so far cleaner, she tried to reassure herself. Safer, maybe. She walked up the step and knocked on the door, Liam and Nora tucked in behind her.

The door was opened suddenly, and a tall, broad man stood in the doorway, looking down at her, frowning.

"I'm looking for a room," she said, her soft Irish lilt obvious.

The frown on the man's face deepened.

"No Irish here," he said, and then slammed the door without giving her a chance to respond.

She stumbled back down the step, feeling her cheeks burn with embarrassment. She'd heard stories of such discrimination, but had assumed that, as a woman on her own with children, somehow she would be safe from it.

Perhaps it was just this one man, she told herself, and walked further down the street. But when she came to the next lodging house, the response was exactly the same—a harsh word, a door slammed— and Katherine and her children were no closer to finding a place to stay.

Katherine was aware that it was getting closer to sunset.

She needed to find somewhere before the night; it wouldn't be safe for them out on the streets.

She'd already taken the bread and cheese from her bag and given it to Liam and Nora, but she knew it wouldn't be long before they'd be hungry again. She started to feel panic grip her. What would she do if she couldn't find somewhere to stay? How could she keep her children safe?

AFTER YET ANOTHER refusal for lodgings Katherine wondered whether moving here had been the right choice after all. She knew she had to leave her home, but now she wondered whether she'd gone too far.

The reactions she'd had so far ranged from suspicious to, at times, openly hostile. As soon as they heard her speak, there was no opportunity to put her case forward—that it was just her and her two children, that they would be no trouble, that she was looking for work, that whatever ideas they might have about her were wrong.

No one wanted to listen. Doors were slammed. And while nothing physical had happened to her, some of the comments made were openly threatening.

When that happened, she would hurry away as

quickly as possible. She had come here to remove herself from danger; there was no way she would put herself in harm's way—at least not knowingly.

When she thought she had no chance of finding lodgings for the night, when it felt like all hope had disappeared and all she could feel was fear and dread in the pit of her stomach, she heard a woman's voice call out to her—an Irish voice—and she turned.

"You'll struggle to find somewhere to stay, here," the woman said kindly. "But I have a room. Come and stay with me. It will be safe for you and your children," she reassured her.

A flood of relief coursed through Katherine.

"Thank you," she said.

"I'm Mary Flynn," the young woman said to her.

"And I'm Katherine Foley, and this is Liam and Nora," she replied, as her son and daughter smiled politely.

"Well, come on then, Katherine Foley—and Liam and Nora—let's get you settled for the night."

Katherine followed Mary further down the street, towards a boarding house that looked worse than any of the others she'd seen so far.

Perhaps this was all she could hope for, she thought. Beggars can't be choosers, she told herself, and followed Mary through the door once she'd opened it, and then up the stairs to the small room that was obviously hers.

It was tidy and clean, and it was clear that Mary was trying to make the best of it—trying to make it feel like a home.

"I've got some extra blankets and pillows," she said. "We can get everyone set up on the floor, seeing as there's just the one bed. Now—let's see what we've got for supper."

KATHERINE SAT in one of the two chairs that Mary had in her room, grateful that she hadn't had to try to find somewhere to sleep on the street with her children that night.

She knew she wouldn't be able to stay with Mary forever, but even having one night of safety—one night where she could rest, gather her thoughts, and try to find a plan for the future she wanted to build for Liam and Nora—meant more than she could say.

The exhaustion overwhelmed her, but as she listened to Mary's sweet Irish voice as she explained to Liam and Nora what she was cooking for supper, Katherine was filled with warmth, and a small spark of hope.

She was sure that Mary had likely faced many

trials since arriving here, many difficulties, and seeing her now, settled and smiling, reassured Katherine that perhaps she too could build a life.

Mary put together a simple stew—some potatoes and vegetables, with the tiniest scraps of meat. How she managed to make it enough for the four of them was impressive, and Katherine thanked her profusely.

It was clear Mary didn't have much, but the fact that she was willing to share the little she had warmed Katherine's heart. Finding someone else from back home helped her to not feel so lonely.

Everything was different here. From the moment she'd stepped off the train, she'd known this wouldn't be easy. She was determined—but that was before door after door had been shut in her face.

She'd been so sure that coming here would mean a fresh start.

No one knew her, no one knew who she was. She was a hard worker, willing to do whatever she needed to provide for her children. But now she wondered whether the fresh start she'd hoped for was going to be so simple after all. The comments that had been made about her being Irish made her realise she'd have to work twice as hard to achieve even half as much.

Once supper was finished and she'd tucked Liam and Nora into bed—doing her best to make the sleeping arrangements as comfortable for them as possible—the two children fell fast asleep.

She knew the exhaustion hadn't been hers alone.

They'd been ripped away from the life they'd always known, from friends and family, and as much as she tried to explain, she knew their young minds didn't truly understand why they were here and why they'd had to go.

She needed to put a plan in place—but for tonight, for now, she needed sleep. Mary seemed to sense that too.

"We'll talk in the morning," she said. "You look exhausted. Get some sleep."

And as Katherine lay down next to her children, stretching out her arm to gather them close, sleep overtook her.

CHAPTER 2

Katherine came to slowly, roused by the gentle whispers of Mary and her two children.

For a moment, she lost herself in the idea that she was still at home—the soft lilt of Irish voices calmed her and drew away the fears that had brought her here.

But she knew she couldn't hide from the reality of her life. There were decisions to be made: a job to be found, lodgings secured—so much to think about.

As she lay there, she recognised how easy it would be to become overwhelmed by it all, and how that overwhelm could lead her to do nothing at all. For now, she remained still, eyes closed, not quite ready to face the day.

She couldn't make out what Mary was saying to Liam and Nora, but the fact that the other woman had taken to them so quickly made her thankful— again—that they'd found each other in a city of so many.

After a few more minutes, Katherine opened her eyes and looked across the room.

Liam and Nora each had a bowl of something in their hands; it was clear Mary had made them breakfast while she'd still been asleep. Mary herself had her hands wrapped around a cup, and Katherine hoped its contents were tea.

She sat up and stretched. Mary smiled at her and, without a word, poured something into another cup and walked it across the room, placing it in Katherine's hands. Katherine was pleased to see it was indeed a cup of tea—just what she needed—and once again, it made her think of home.

MARY WALKED BACK over to where the children sat, encouraging them to finish the food she had prepared for them.

Katherine saw that she'd also made them a hot drink, and once they had finished the contents of their bowls, they both began drinking, glancing over at their mother from over the cups.

Katherine could sense the ripple of fear that they both felt, and she reminded herself once again that moving them here had been for all of their safety.

She pushed away the memories from the previous day—the memory of people slamming doors in their faces, of not being able to find somewhere to stay.

She refused to believe that everyone could be the same.

They'd found Mary, hadn't they? Or at least Mary had found them. And as Katherine looked around the room in the dim light of morning, it was clear once again that Mary had managed to build some kind of life for herself here, even amongst the discrimination her Irishness seemed to cause.

Katherine knew she would be able to do the same.

She finished her tea, took a deep breath, and stood up, folding the blankets that had been their bed for the night and placing them in a pile.

She walked over to where Mary and the children were and sat down in the chair near the small fireplace.

She'd never known Liam and Nora to be so quiet.

"Thank you, Mary," Katherine said. "I'm not sure what we would have done, or where we would have stayed, if you hadn't helped us."

"Oh, you would have done the same," Mary replied. "It's not easy here. Not for us."

Katherine nodded.

It wasn't just about being Irish, but also about being women.

There was so much to think about to keep themselves safe. It wasn't something Katherine was naïve to—she'd learnt the hard way, and she was determined never to find herself in that situation again.

"You can stay here as long as you need," Mary said.

"I appreciate that," Katherine replied, though it was clear the tiny room couldn't hold the four of them for very long.

And while she was truly grateful for Mary's offer, she didn't want to outstay her welcome.

"I need to find work," Katherine said. "Do you know anywhere?"

She looked at Mary hopefully, aware of just how much she now relied on this young woman she barely knew.

"I work in a button factory," Mary said. "It doesn't offer much in the way of wages, but it's something—

and there's always work. They'd have you working non-stop if they could. There's a few of us Irish girls there, and I'm sure I can get you on."

Katherine had done a lot of different jobs— mostly cleaning, some sewing and mending—things she could manage around her children.

The idea of working in a factory for hours on end made her heart sink, but she knew she had no choice. She needed to do whatever she could to provide for the three of them, and so she nodded at Mary's suggestion.

"Some of the other girls bring their children," Mary added, "and as long as they're quiet and no trouble, the owner seems to be fine with it." She turned and smiled at Nora and Liam. "And I'm sure you two will be no trouble at all," she said gently.

The two of them nodded their heads quickly, and Katherine couldn't help the soft smile that rose to her lips.

They were good children—no trouble at all—and she would give everything for them. If that meant working in some terrible factory, then so be it.

"I go back into work this afternoon," Mary said. "Come with me, then. I'll speak to the owner, but I don't think there'll be any problems."

Katherine nodded in agreement.

There was nothing to say, really, and it was yet another thing to be grateful for. After so much rejection, it was starting to feel as though Mary was some kind of guardian angel placed in her path.

"Now, the two of you stay quiet," Katherine whispered again to Liam and Nora. "Stay close."

They had gone with Mary to the button factory where she worked, and Katherine and the children were waiting just inside the door as Mary walked over to speak with the owner.

She was too far away for Katherine to hear what was being said, but she watched as Mary and the owner spoke, then looked over toward her. They exchanged a few more words before Mary nodded and came back to where Katherine and the children stood.

"Come on now," Mary said. "I told you it'd be no trouble getting you work here." She smiled, but Katherine caught a shadow in her eyes, as though she wasn't being told the full truth.

Still, she was too grateful for the opportunity to ask questions.

She walked over to the owner with Mary, keeping Liam and Nora tucked in close at her side.

He grunted at her as she stood before him and looked her up and down. She didn't like the look in his eyes, but she knew she had to earn money, and her choices were limited.

"Work hard and keep those children out of trouble," he said gruffly. "Mary here'll show you what you need to do."

Then he turned and walked away, not sparing her a backward glance.

As the air escaped her, Katherine realised she'd been holding her breath.

"Come on," Mary said gently, guiding her over to where the other women were seated.

The rest of her day was spent learning the tasks she'd be doing.

It wasn't difficult work, but Katherine was sure it would become mind-numbing after a while.

Thankfully, the group of women she was placed with were all Irish. Even in this place where she felt so alone, they seemed a piece of home.

They welcomed her easily, and the gentle sound of their Irish voices chatting as they worked soothed her, taking her mind off the worries that never seemed to drift far.

. . .

KATHERINE WAS surprised at how quickly the day passed. Before she'd realised, everyone was packing up and getting ready to go home.

The women she'd spent time with had spoken often of how difficult it had been to find both work and somewhere to stay.

It worried Katherine—perhaps the life she had planned for herself and her children would be harder to build than she had originally thought.

As if sensing her anxiety, Mary rested a gentle hand on her arm.

"Just as I said this morning, Katherine—you and the children can stay with me for as long as you need. Just focus on the work for now. I'll help you find a place when you're ready."

Katherine smiled at Mary gratefully.

She was thankful for the other woman's support, but she also knew she had to build a home for herself, for Nora, and for Liam—and that home wasn't sleeping on the floor in Mary's room.

WHILE IT WASN'T the home that Katherine had imagined for herself or her children, over the next few weeks that's what it became and in a strange way it even started to feel like home.

Mary helped her to look after the children and Katherine did what she could to help make meals and keep Mary's small room tidy.

They seemed to find an easy rhythm between them between doing that and working at the button factory and so when they returned to the lodging house, from the factory one evening it came as some surprise when Mary learned that a room just near hers had become available.

She spoke to the owner on Katherine's behalf, and when she came back to her own room to share the news, Katherine could hardly believe how much had changed in what seemed to be such a short time.

She'd gone from fearing that being Irish would mean she'd never be able to build the life she'd hoped for, to suddenly having a job and now a room they could call their own. Not to mention the friendships that she had made.

It was as if Mary truly were some kind of guardian angel—her presence seemed to smooth the path ahead.

Katherine pulled the other woman into a tight hug.

"I'll never forget everything you've done for me and for mine," she said. "I'm forever in your debt."

When she stepped back, she noticed Mary's

cheeks had flushed red. She mumbled something under her breath, embarrassed.

"No, really, Mary—if it wasn't for you, I'd hate to think where we'd be. You've done so much to help us. Thank you."

As Katherine guided the children into the room they would now call home, she could feel her spirits start to lift.

She knew that coming here had been the right thing to do—that this would be a fresh start, a place of safety. And now, it seemed, everything was finally falling into place.

BUT THE NEXT MORNING, when Katherine woke, her heart faltered as she looked over, towards her children, where they were tucked up in bed still asleep.

Liam's hair, messy and falling into his face, made him look almost like a baby again.

But it was Nora who caused the blood in Katherine's veins to chill.

Nora's hair was stuck to her face, damp and limp, her cheeks red, and when Katherine reached over to place her hand gently on the girl's forehead, she could feel the heat coming off her before she had even touched her skin.

The peace she had felt the evening before, when everything had seemed to be starting to fall into place, came back to haunt her now as she looked at Nora, knowing that her little girl was unwell.

Liam stirred beside his sister, but Nora didn't move, and even when Katherine gave her a gentle shake and the little girl finally awoke, it was obvious that she struggled to open her eyes.

When Katherine asked her how she felt, the little girl squeaked out that her throat hurt, that her head hurt, that the daylight hurt her eyes, and that she just wanted to go back to sleep because she was so, so very tired.

It felt like a tight hand gripped Katherine's heart as she watched her little girl fall back to sleep almost as soon as she had finished speaking.

Now it wasn't just putting a roof over their heads and food on the table that she needed to provide — she somehow needed to find the medical care that Nora required to make her well again. Once more, she knew she would have to rely on Mary. After tucking Nora back beneath the blankets and settling Liam at the small table with a simple breakfast, Katherine made her way to Mary's room, hoping that the other woman would be able to help.

CHAPTER 3

*K*atherine sat in the small room, her eyes focused on the floor as she did everything she could not to look at the other women surrounding her.

Some were here because they were obviously unwell themselves, but many were like her, their faces gripped with fear for what might happen to the child either wrapped in their arms or sitting by their side.

Mary had known exactly where they needed to go. *They want to be paid,* Mary had told her, and Katherine knew that, of course.

She had a small amount of money left and hoped and prayed that it would be enough—or that she might be able to pay back whatever was required from her meagre wages. All she knew was that she needed Nora to get better.

The little girl sat next to her, leaning in, her eyes closed, probably asleep. The short walk here, where Katherine had half-carried her, had taken what little energy the child had left.

Katherine looked down at her, doing her best to brush the hair from her forehead, but the sweat that had glistened on her face from the moment Katherine had woken her seemed heavier than ever, her hair sticking to her skin.

Her face was redder, and Katherine could feel the heat from her little girl's body through her own clothing.

She hadn't been able to get her to eat anything before they'd left the boarding house room—only small sips of water that Katherine had tried to coax into her.

The fear that had gripped her that morning hadn't passed; if anything, as she watched her little girl and saw how ill she was becoming, a slight panic began to rise in her chest.

She's going to see a doctor, she reminded herself. *They will be able to help.*

Whatever she needed to pay, she would find the money.

She would borrow it, even steal it, though that went against everything she believed in.

But for her children—for her daughter, for Nora —she would do whatever it took.

Mary was looking after Liam, having taken him to work with her that morning.

She had said she would make it right with the owner of the button factory, but already Katherine was aware that not being there would mean her already small wage at the end of the week would be even smaller.

She pushed the thought away. There was nothing she could do about it right now.

All her energy, all her thoughts, needed to be focused on the little girl by her side.

When it was finally Katherine's turn to take Nora into the even smaller room where the doctor waited, the waiting area had become standing room only.

It seemed that no sooner did people leave than more came to take their place.

She thought back to the home she had left—the small village, the fresh air and open spaces.

Even there, people became ill suddenly; even there, people were lost to those they loved; even there, children... Katherine pushed that last thought away. Even back home, illness had followed everyone around.

Then it was no wonder that there were so many people sitting here waiting to see the doctor. The city she had moved to had people everywhere, animals everywhere—everything seemed slightly uncared for—so it was no wonder that the room she was in was so full.

She closed the door on it and walked over to the small table where the doctor sat behind it, looking at her.

He also looked exhausted, but then, given the number of people waiting to see him and the number he had already seen, it was really no wonder.

He looked young—older than her, but somehow she had expected an older man to be sitting where he was.

He smiled at her kindly, and she could see that even through his tiredness he was trying to set her at ease.

. . .

KATHERINE PLACED Nora on the chair beside her and did her best to try to wake the little girl up.

"SHE'S BEEN like this since this morning," she said. "She'll barely wake. She's eaten nothing, had only a few sips of water, and her skin is burning to the touch. She says her throat hurts, her head hurts, and the light's too bright."

KATHERINE'S GAZE hadn't left Nora as she explained to the doctor, but now she turned to him, knowing that the panic and worry she felt were clearly written on her face.

"Well, let's take a look at her. Why don't you pop her up on the examination table over there, and we'll see what we can do," his voice was just as kind as the smile he had given her.

In any other situation, Katherine was sure that she would have found it reassuring—that it would have made her confident that no matter what, he would be able to make her little girl well again.

But at this moment in time, Katherine allowed the fear of what might be to overtake her.

SHE BLINKED BACK tears and took a few slow, deep breaths, trying to calm her racing heart.

She had come all this way for a new life, a fresh start, to get away from the danger that had found her back home—and now she wondered whether all she had done was jump from the boiling pot into the very fire itself.

THE IDEA that trying to find safety by coming here had ended up putting her little girl in mortal danger was more than she could bear. She had promised herself that she would do whatever it took to give her children a good life, to look after them, to make sure they were happy—and yet here Nora was, lying on a small table, looking tiny and frail, and Katherine had never felt more helpless.

What was worse was that she had had to hand over all the money she had saved to get to this very point. Just having the doctor look over Nora had cost her everything she had.

. . .

SHE WATCHED as he examined her little girl. He was gentle, speaking to her in a kind, hushed voice.

Surely he would help her, no matter what.

But when he turned and walked back to his desk and sat down, she could see him writing, at least, on a small piece of paper.

"These medicines will help her," he said. "If you go to the apothecary, they'll be able to give you everything you need. I've written it out clearly and they'll let you know the dosages, of course. She'll need rest, you'll need to keep a close eye on her, make sure she drinks, and try to get her to eat some-thing—some vegetables, some kind of broth—things that would be easy."

Katherine's heart dropped into her stomach as she listened to his words—all very sensible—and how on earth was she to pay for any of it?

DID he not see the world outside of this room?

Could he not tell from looking at her that what he obviously thought was very simple was so far out of her reach?

. . .

SHE TOOK the piece of paper that he handed to her and nodded. What could she possibly say?

SHE PICKED UP NORA, holding her carefully in her arms.

"THANK YOU, DOCTOR," she said.

It was the only thing that came to mind.

INSIDE, she felt like she was screaming.

She didn't even bother to look at the list he had given her, folding it quickly and stuffing it into a pocket before leaving the room and walking through the waiting area, which had become even busier than before.

She walked back to the boarding house in a daze. How on earth would she pay for medicines? Where would she find the money for vegetables and broth?

HOW COULD she possibly look after a little girl if she had to be at work—and she *had* to go to work if she had even a hope of paying for anything Nora required to make her better.

She had thought that the doctor would give her medicine—that the money she had paid to see him would include something, something that would help her daughter get better—and the helplessness she had felt seeing Nora on that examination table only intensified.

She became more aware of the fact that she couldn't provide anything to help her little girl.

When she got back to her room, she tucked Nora back into bed, having encouraged her to drink a little more water, but no sooner did Nora's head hit the pillow than she was fast asleep once again.

Katherine sat and watched as the little girl slept. Her breaths seemed to rasp in her chest, and every now and then she would cough—and Katherine knew that she was getting worse.

. . .

AND THAT WAS how Mary found her, when she walked in with Liam by her side.

As soon as she saw her son, Katherine looked him over, desperate to see whether the illness that had overcome Nora was evident in him.

But no — the little boy talked endlessly about the day he'd had with Mary and the other women. His easy smile, his sweet voice — which in any other situation would have brought a smile to Katherine's face — failed to lift her spirits. All she could think about was that her little girl was desperately unwell, and there was nothing she could do about it.

Mary did her best to ease her concern, making a broth with what vegetables she had and helping Katherine as they both sat Nora up and coaxed her to take a small bowlful.

But there was nothing that Mary could do about the list of medicines the doctor had given them.

"I'm going to have to take her to work with me tomorrow," Katherine said. "I have no choice. I can't afford to lose this job, and I can't afford not to be making any money. I have no idea how much all of these medicines will cost me, but it's going to be far more than I have," she sighed deeply, "probably far more than I could ever earn. But I'll do everything I can."

Mary reached over, placing a hand over hers.

"I know you will. And I'll help you in whatever way I can too."

"I can't ask you to do any more than you have, Mary. I wouldn't have got this far without you, and I'm so grateful. But this is my responsibility, and I will find a way. Thank you."

Mary said her goodbyes and went back to her own room, and Katherine felt the loss of the woman who had so quickly become such a close friend.

But she had meant everything that she had said — she would do whatever was needed. And tomorrow, she needed to go to work.

She would bundle Nora up as best she could, and she would make sure that no one knew how unwell she was, especially the overseers in the factory.

She hoped they wouldn't make her leave.

Once she had tucked Liam into bed, she sat by the small fire, looking into the flames, trying to think of ways she might earn some extra money.

She could sew, she could clean — there were so many things she was willing to do. But she was aware that there were only so many hours in a day, and all the work she could find would barely earn her anything.

She knew there were plenty of women just like

herself, doing everything they could to scrape together enough to look after themselves and their children. That had been all too evident in the doctor's waiting room that day.

Just as she had sat there, full of worry and concern for her child, she had been surrounded by mothers doing exactly the same — all of them probably now sitting just as she was, trying to think of ways to provide what was needed to make their children well again.

She took herself to bed, closing her eyes but knowing that sleep would probably not come. Her mind raced. Yet, surprisingly, when morning came, she realised that she must have eventually dropped off.

She lay in bed, knowing she needed to get up, listening to Liam's gentle breathing. Compared to Nora's — the in and out of her breath was raspy and loud.

Just as Katherine was about to rise, the little girl was overcome with coughing.

Katherine hurried to get some water, helping Nora to take a few sips. Her eyes remained closed, almost as if she were still asleep, and Katherine felt a mixture of dread — knowing how unwell she was — followed quickly by fierce protectiveness.

She would go to work today.

She would see if she could work more hours. She would ask the other women if they knew of any small jobs she might be able to do, preferably here in her room, so she wouldn't have to leave her children or take them to yet another place. She was sure she could find something. There had to be more that she could do.

She took a deep breath, pushing the fear aside, replacing it with determination.

She hadn't come this far to lose it all without fighting.

CHAPTER 4

*J*ust as she had thought, the other women at the button factory had plenty of ideas about ways Katherine might earn some extra money, but none of them were any different from the things Katherine had already considered.

They were simple, small jobs, none paying very well, and Katherine had no idea how she might make enough.

SHE HAD EVEN GONE SO FAR as to visit the apothecary with the list from the doctor, asking how much each of the items would cost. The man behind the counter gave her amounts that were far beyond anything she could ever imagine affording.

She found herself begging him, hoping he might take pity on her and her daughter, but his harsh face and even harsher words made it clear that there was no charity to be found here — no kindness, no help.

GRABBING the list from the counter, Katherine had hurried out of the door as tears of worry and frustration rolled down her cheeks.

She remembered the doctor's kind face and had somehow thought she might find that same kindness here, but it was plain that was not to be.

AS SHE STUMBLED out onto the street, not looking where she was going, she felt strong hands grip her arms as she almost fell.

"Thank you," she stuttered, looking up into the face of a man who looked vaguely familiar.

She blinked away her tears and quickly rubbed her cheeks dry.

Then she remembered — she had seen him at the button factory where she worked.

He was not an owner or an overseer, nor did he

work there himself, but it was clear he had some dealings with the proprietor, and she had seen him there a few times.

SHE RECALLED FEELING his eyes on her from a distance while she worked, though she had thought nothing of it at the time.

Now, as he looked down at her, it was clear he recognised her as well.

Once she was steady on her feet, he dropped his hands and took a step back, smiling at her — but there was no kindness in it, not like the doctor's smile, she thought.

"THANK YOU," she said again and made to walk around him.

"Katherine, isn't it?" he said.

"YES, SIR," she nodded.

"I hear you have an unwell child — your daughter."

. . .

KATHERINE NODDED AGAIN, unsure where this conversation was leading.

It seemed word had spread quickly around the factory.

Of course, she had spoken to many of the women about her situation, asking for their advice, but she had not imagined that a man like the one standing before her would have heard the women's chatter.

"I've heard that you're looking for some work," he continued. "I imagine medicines to help your daughter are expensive. I can help you," he said.

Katherine felt her skin crawl, suddenly aware of what he might be proposing.

Without realising it, she drew back a few steps. As if he had read her mind, he gave a quiet laugh.

"NO, NOT LIKE THAT," he said.

IT WAS HARD NOT to notice a small flash of disgust in his eyes, and Katherine could not decide whether she was relieved or humiliated.

"We can discuss it another time," he said, "but I do genuinely want to help you."

. . .

He smiled again, then said goodbye and walked away.

Katherine turned and watched him go, wondering what he had meant. If he had heard about the conversations she'd had, perhaps it was just cleaning or sewing work he was offering.

Still, she felt uneasy about him as she turned and made her way back to the boarding house, where Mary had kindly offered to look after Liam and Nora while she was out.

Perhaps this gentleman could help her, she thought, realising that she did not even know his name.

She would listen to what he had to say, she told herself, and wondered when he might come to speak to her again.

She was almost surprised when he caught her attention the very next day.

She had just arrived at the button factory, having

settled Nora comfortably and given Liam something to keep him busy so she could work.

HE MOTIONED for her to come over to where he stood slightly to one side, and she realised he was trying not to draw attention to himself — or to the two of them together.

"So", he said to her, "Would you like my help?"

"What kind of help are you offering, sir?" she said, wary.

He still hadn't told her his name, and Katherine was unsure whether she could ask him.

"I have some work. You could earn some money," he said. "Good money. Enough to buy the medicine you need for your little girl."

Katherine's heart raced at the thought that she might be able to provide everything Nora needed to make her better again.

But she knew that good money wasn't made from sewing, or cleaning, or working more hours here at the button factory.

She remembered the glint of disgust she had seen flash in his eyes when she had thought he was proposing that she sell herself, and so she was sure that it wasn't that, either.

Gathering her courage, she asked him his name.

"I DON'T EVEN KNOW who you are, sir," she said, "never mind what it is that you might ask me to do."

"Marcus Denton", he replied, and smiled.

He was handsome when he smiled, she realised, but she felt a wariness, an unease.

That, behind his handsome exterior, there was some kind of darkness.

Yet she could not deny that she needed the money.

Nora seemed to be fading before her very eyes; every now and then it would seem as though she took a turn for the better, and Katherine's heart would calm.

But just as she thought her little girl was improving, she would be awoken in the night by the hacking cough and wheezing as her daughter struggled for every breath.

Katherine stood, looking at the gentleman before her — Marcus Denton — and waited.

As if sensing her uncertainty, he put out his hand,

offering it to her, and she placed her smaller hand in his.

She could feel his warmth, but it did nothing to ease the feeling she had.

If it were not for her desperation, she knew she ought to have turned and run — run as far as she could from the man.

"Perhaps we could find some time, and I could explain what it is that I'm offering," he said to her.

And knowing that she truly had no choice, Katherine agreed to meet with Mr Denton once she had finished work.

She spoke to Mary, asking if she could keep an eye on Nora and Liam for her.

Mary had obvious questions in her eyes, but she agreed.

Katherine was unsure how much to share with the other woman; if the work offered good money, then she knew, without a doubt, that the chances of it being legal were slim.

Mary had been good to them, and the last thing Katherine wanted was to drag her into something that might get her into trouble.

She did her best to mumble something that sounded plausible as a reason, and then made her way to the small café that Marcus Denton had told her to go to.

SHE COULD SEE him sitting at a table through the window, and even now, as she had her hand on the door, she hesitated.

She'd done everything she could to keep herself and her children out of trouble, to keep them safe.

She'd moved away from everything she'd known, from all those that she'd loved, to do exactly that – and yet here she was, once again questioning the wisdom of what she was about to do.

But the truth was that no matter how many hours she did at the button factory, no matter how many small jobs of sewing, no matter how much cleaning she undertook, the medicine required for Nora cost more money than she could ever hope to earn — or certainly earn quickly enough.

Whatever the risk, she would do it.

She walked through the door and made her way over to the table where Marcus Denton was waiting for her.

"I'm glad you came," he said. "I've got us some tea."

As she sat, watching him, he poured her a cup before pouring his own.

. . .

EVERY NOW AND then he would look up and smile at her, and each time she felt a grip of concern. But she sat and waited, sipping her tea, ready to hear what it was that he had to say.

"There's an exhibition in the city," he said. "I'm sure you're aware of it."

Katherine nodded.

"I've got some items," he said carefully, "and there are people coming along to the exhibition who want those items. It's not something I can handle myself. But you, Katherine — no one would be looking at someone like you."

While he smiled down at her as he spoke the words, she knew exactly what he was saying.

Someone of her class was unlikely to draw attention, especially if she were surrounded by well-dressed, beautiful women.

She did her best to brush off the implied insult.

"So really, I'm just looking for a courier of sorts," he said. "Do you think that's something you could do?"

Katherine had no doubt that she was capable of whatever he was asking.

But it was clear that whatever items he was talking about were stolen; she wasn't naïve.

It was this awareness that brought her up short. Was this really something she wanted to be a part of?

When she'd considered the possibility of having to steal the money required she hadn't thought too much about what that might look like.

She knew that it probably would been risky but this, what Marcus Denton was suggesting was a whole other level of risk and possible danger.

Not only the risk of being caught but she felt that there was the risk from Marcus Denton himself and while she wasn't sure what that risk might be, it filled her with unease.

What would that risk mean for her? What would it mean for her children?

"You don't need to decide now," he said to her, standing and barely touching his own cup of tea.

He took out his pocket watch, glanced at the time, then replaced it before looking down at her once more.

"But don't leave it too long," he added. "Nora's not looking well."

Leaving those words hanging between them, he walked towards the door and out of the café, passing the window where she sat, without giving her a backward glance.

Katherine poured herself another cup of tea, her hands shaking slightly as she realised that, no matter the risk, no matter her fears, the predicament she faced left her no choice but to accept the offer that Marcus Denton had placed before her.

CHAPTER 5

❦

*E*ven though Katherine felt backed into a corner and believed she had no choice but to become involved in Marcus Denton's illegal dealings, she still spent the next few days trying to find another way to earn the money for Nora's medicine.

She watched her daughter closely, searching for any sign that her health was improving.

She tried to tell herself that if she just waited a little longer, Nora would be fine—that she didn't have to go down this path.

But Nora remained unwell, the colour still drained from her cheeks, the fever ever lurking beneath her damp skin.

Katherine longed for someone to talk to about it,

and while she knew she could trust Mary, she didn't want to draw her into anything dangerous.

Mary had become her friend—the closest person to her and her little family in this new life—and the thought that anything Katherine might do could bring trouble to her was unbearable.

So Katherine stayed quiet, letting the constant thoughts tumble through her mind—the pros and cons of the situation—until eventually, sheer exhaustion and the realisation that this was the only real option available to properly care for Nora led her to seek out Marcus Denton, ready to tell him she would do what he needed.

He nodded at her as if he'd expected no other response other than the quiet *yes* that she gave him.

When the appointed evening came, she slipped away from the lodging house under the pretence of running errands.

Mary didn't press her, though Katherine saw the curiosity in her friend's eyes. She promised herself that once this was over—once Nora was better—she would explain everything.

Marcus met her just beyond the market square, near the back of a quiet public house. He didn't speak immediately, just nodded to her and pressed a small parcel into her gloved hands.

"Take it to this address," he said, giving her a folded slip of paper. "Hand it to the man who answers. Say nothing else."

Katherine felt like this was some kind of test and she looked down at the package—wrapped in plain brown paper and tied with twine—and felt the weight of it, not only in her hands, but also somewhere in her chest.

It wasn't heavy, but it felt loaded with meaning and she did her best to ignore what that was.

She nodded once, tucking the note into her apron pocket, and turned away, her heart pounding in her chest.

The walk through the city streets felt endless.

Her eyes darted from stranger to stranger, watching for anyone who might look too closely, anyone who might ask questions. Every step felt like one closer to disaster. She whispered a silent prayer with each footfall, willing herself not to be noticed. It was just a parcel. Just a delivery. Nothing more.

When she reached the address, a small door tucked between two darkened shops, she knocked once, as Marcus had instructed. A narrow-eyed man opened it and took the parcel from her hands without a word. He disappeared back into the shadows and closed the door. That was it. It was over.

Katherine stood there for a moment, unsure what to feel. She had half expected someone to leap out and grab her—to accuse her, to arrest her. But nothing happened. No one paid her any mind. She turned and walked away.

Marcus was waiting in the same alley. He gave her a small smile and handed her a handful of coins. The sight of them made her stomach twist. She accepted them silently, tucked them into her pocket, and left.

BACK AT THE LODGING HOUSE, she sat by Nora's side, watching her sleep. In the dim candlelight, her daughter's face looked less flushed, her breathing less laboured. The medicine she'd been able to buy from the apothecary that afternoon had already begun to help. Katherine clung to that small glimmer of hope like a lifeline.

Still, guilt gnawed at her. She couldn't bring herself to tell Mary what she had done. She tried to reassure herself that as soon as Nora was better then she wouldn't need to do it again—that the work at the button factory would be enough to continue caring for her children without further dishonesty.

But that evening, as she washed after work before starting to prepare the evening meal, Marcus's words echoed in her ears.

"You did well," he had said. "We'll need you again soon."

And she hadn't said no or made it clear that she wouldn't be doing this forever.

THE FOLLOWING MORNING, as she gathered a shawl around her shoulders and prepared to take the children outside for a bit of fresh air, Nora collapsed.

One moment the child was standing beside her, the next she had crumpled to the ground, her body folding in on itself like a rag doll. Panic surged through Katherine. She knelt quickly, cradling Nora's head in her lap.

People passed by without stopping.

Some glanced over with mild interest; others averted their eyes. Katherine's voice shook as she called out for help, trying not to scream.

It was Mary's voice that rose above the noise.

"Someone—please, she needs a doctor!"

Just as Katherine thought she might have to carry her daughter all the way to the surgery herself, a gentleman approached through the crowd. He was tall, his coat neat but plain, his face serious and composed.

"I'm a physician," he said, crouching beside them. "Henry Ellsworth."

He examined Nora gently, brushing her hair back, checking her pulse, placing the back of his hand against her forehead. He asked questions—about her illness, her fever, the medicine.

Katherine answered as best she could, though her voice caught more than once.

When he gathered Nora in his arms and stood, asking Katherine where they lived, her heart stuttered and she felt heat rush into her cheeks at the thought of taking him to her lodging house.

"She needs rest," he said finally. "And more treatment. Let me help you get her back home and then may I visit you later, bring some things that might help?"

Katherine hesitated.

A doctor.

A stranger.

Yet his hands had been kind, his tone compassionate, and there had been no judgement in his gaze.

"Yes," she said softly. "Please."

She led him to the lodging house and up the stairs to her room, leaving the door open as he placed Nora on the bed gently.

He nodded and gave her a brief smile.

"I'll call round before dusk," he said, and walked back downstairs.

Katherine watched him from the window as he left the lodging house and crossed the road before vanishing into the crowd with quiet efficiency.

Katherine turned and looked down at Nora as she lay on the bed, her face pale.

As she stood there Mary walked in holding Liam's hand and speaking quietly to him. Katherine could only imagine how frightened the little boy had been at seeing how ill his sister was.

She gathered her son into her arms trying to stop the trembling in her own body as she tried to silently reassure him.

She thought about Marcus Denton and what she'd done for him to pay for Nora's medicine.

"You did what you had to," she told herself. "You got her medicine. You helped her. That's all that matters."

She had hoped that she wouldn't have to do any more of the couriering that he'd asked her to do. She'd hoped that Nora was well enough and that her interactions with Marcus Denton would be coming to an end.

But now she wasn't sure if that would be possible.

THAT EVENING, Dr Ellsworth returned as promised.

He came with a satchel of remedies and instructions, careful and clear. He refused payment when Katherine offered what little she had left.

"I know what it's like," he said simply. "To be desperate. Let this be my kindness."

After he left, Katherine sat in silence, watching Nora sleep.

The doctor's help had been freely given, warm and honest.

It was everything Marcus Denton's dealings were not. And yet, Nora's improving health was due to both men.

She felt torn between gratitude and guilt, trapped in a place where the right path and the necessary one no longer aligned.

That night, she didn't sleep. She sat by the window, the city's shadows stretching long across the floor, and wondered if she had already begun to lose herself in the choices she had made.

CHAPTER 6

*T*he streets bustled with early morning tradesmen as Katherine slipped quietly through the back gate of the boarding house, a parcel secured beneath her shawl.

Her steps were quick and deliberate, each footfall echoing louder than she liked in the cobbled alleyway behind the apothecary.

The city was still drowsy, its upper windows just beginning to light with the day, but Katherine's thoughts raced. She'd done this run before, three times now. Each time it became harder to justify.

She told herself the money was for Nora.

And it was.

But the act—the delivery, the secretive nature, the constant fear—it was eating into her. Every time

Marcus handed her a new parcel, the same sickening churn unfurled in her stomach.

She was becoming something she had once promised herself she would never be. But what choice did she have?

The coins in her pocket clinked with her hurried pace. Enough for vegetables. Enough for broth. Enough for the tinctures Henry Ellsworth recommended.

Henry.

He had been calling by regularly now, always unannounced, always with a quiet knock at the door and a kind smile.

Nora was stronger with each visit.

Her eyes had regained a touch of their sparkle, and she was walking again, albeit with a little unsteadiness.

It made Katherine's heart lift—but that lift brought with it a deep ache of guilt.

She'd told Henry only part of the truth.

That she was working extra hours. That she'd taken in mending for the factory girls.

She hadn't told him about the parcels. About Marcus Denton.

Henry had noticed the wear on her face though.

"Buy what you can manage," he'd said just yesterday, after examining Nora's breathing with the stethoscope he always carried. "The right food will go a long way. Broth, root vegetables. And eggs, if you can afford them."

She had nodded, thanking him with quiet sincerity.

And then she'd gone back to the alley behind the public house where Marcus was waiting, leaned against the wall like the city itself owed him something.

He knew exactly where her money was going.

He smiled too easily, his expression always slightly too knowing.

"You see, Katherine," he'd said, his tone syrupy, "I'm not such a villain. I'm helping you help her. Isn't that what you wanted?"

And what could she say?

He had her trapped—bound by her own desperation.

THAT MORNING, with the latest job completed, Katherine made her way toward the market.

She bought carrots, a cabbage, a small cut of mutton too stringy to tempt anyone else.

She even managed to find a woman selling six

eggs for a fair price, and when she handed over the coins, a strange rush of satisfaction swept through her.

Food. Real food.

She returned to the boarding house just as Mary was ushering Liam down the stairs.

"I was going to send him to find you," Mary said with a soft look. "He was getting anxious."

"I didn't mean to be gone long," Katherine said, brushing a hand through Liam's hair. "Thank you for looking out for him."

"You know you don't have to thank me." Mary hesitated. "Though... I worry sometimes. You're tired. Thinner than when you came. Just... be careful."

Katherine nodded, managing a faint smile.

"I'll rest when I can. But for now, there's broth to be made."

Inside their small room, Nora sat upright in bed, playing quietly with a scrap of embroidery thread and a wooden spool.

Her cheeks were no longer flushed red with fever, and the circles beneath her eyes had faded from purple to pale grey.

She looked up as Katherine entered, her smile a little crooked but warm.

"I'm not as tired today," she said. "Can I sit by the fire later?"

"Of course," Katherine said. "We'll have our supper there."

She prepared the broth slowly, letting the scent of meat and vegetables fill the room.

It was simple, but hearty, and when Nora ate a full bowl without complaint, Katherine felt her eyes sting with tears she had no intention of shedding.

THAT EVENING, Henry arrived again.

He always seemed to come at dusk, just as the lamplighters passed along the street. He checked Nora's pulse, her throat, listened carefully to her breathing.

"She's doing better," he said, glancing over his shoulder at Katherine. "Your care is what's saving her."

Katherine looked away, her face flushing.

After he'd left, Liam curled into her lap and fell asleep mid-sentence, and Katherine sat staring into the fire. But the warmth didn't reach her bones.

Her nerves were stretched taut, humming with the weight of too many secrets.

. . .

MARCUS CAME for her three days later, earlier than expected.

"There's a shipment this week," he said, stepping inside the stairwell of the boarding house. "Larger than usual. I need someone reliable."

"You said these were small deliveries," Katherine said quietly. "Not… bigger things."

His smile didn't falter.

"You're reliable. And you're smart. I wouldn't ask if I didn't think you could handle it."

"But what if someone sees me?"

"They won't. You're careful. That's why I trust you."

Trust. What a word to use.

He meant she was desperate. And desperate people didn't say no.

Katherine clenched her hands.

"I have children. If anything goes wrong…"

Marcus's expression darkened slightly.

"Nothing will go wrong. Unless, of course, you'd prefer to stop entirely. But I'd hate to think of what that might mean for your daughter's recovery."

It was a threat dressed in velvet. She heard it clearly.

She said nothing, only nodded.

She would go. Again.

· · ·

THE NEXT EVENING, under cover of fog and soot-stained mist, Katherine slipped into the east side of the city. The air there smelled of coal and stale beer.

Marcus had given her a different parcel this time —heavier, harder to conceal.

She hid it beneath the folds of her skirt, tying her shawl tightly around her shoulders.

She was halfway down Lark Lane when she saw the constables.

They weren't moving with urgency, but there were two of them—broad-shouldered men in dark uniforms—and they were checking crates behind the grocer's shop.

Her stomach turned.

She ducked into a nearby alley, holding her breath, her hands slick with sweat.

One of the constables turned slightly, looking down the alley, but didn't come forward.

He seemed uninterested. Or unaware.

Still, Katherine waited until her legs began to ache before she dared move again.

When she finally delivered the parcel to a sour-faced man near the docks, her hands were trembling.

Her heart hadn't stopped hammering since the moment she'd seen the uniformed men.

She left with barely a word and didn't notice the chill in the air until she reached the boarding house. Her hands were numb by then, her body stiff with fear and cold.

Mary met her at the door.

"Katherine?" she asked quietly. "What's wrong?"

"Nothing," Katherine replied quickly. "Just tired."

But even as she said it, she knew Mary didn't believe her.

THE NEXT DAY, Henry brought more good news.

"She's turning a corner," he said, after listening carefully to Nora's lungs. "Another few days, and I think she'll be properly on her feet again."

Katherine closed her eyes, relief flooding through her. She reached out, took his hand briefly.

"Thank you. Truly."

Henry hesitated.

"I've been meaning to ask… Have you considered finding something less demanding than the factory? You look worn to the bone."

"I do what I must," she said quietly. "The work pays."

"Barely," he murmured. "There are other ways. Some safer than others."

Katherine looked at him sharply, trying to read his face.

"You think I've done something wrong?"

"No," he said, but his tone suggested he suspected more than he said aloud. "Only that you deserve help. And if you ever need it—ask."

She nodded, but her throat was tight.

She was not accustomed to kindness that didn't come with a price.

THAT NIGHT, after Nora had fallen asleep and Liam lay snoring softly under his blanket, Katherine sat staring at the coins she had hidden in a tin beneath the floorboards.

The same coins that had bought the food.

The medicine.

That had paid for coal and thread and the mended stockings on Nora's feet.

The same coins that now burned in her palm like judgement.

She thought of Marcus's words—smooth, dangerous.

She thought of Henry's eyes—honest, concerned.

And she realised with growing unease that she was no longer sure who she was becoming.

The next day, she refused Marcus's knock. She didn't answer the stairwell door. She didn't leave the boarding house.

He didn't call again that day.

But she knew he would. She knew this wasn't over.

And as she watched her daughter take slow, sure steps across the room, Katherine understood that her choices had changed something fundamental.

The question wasn't whether she would go back to Marcus.

The question was how long she could afford not to.

CHAPTER 7

*K*atherine had never considered herself a woman prone to sentiment, but something had shifted in her since Henry's visits began.

It wasn't merely gratitude for the doctor's care of Nora—though that in itself would have been enough—it was the way he listened. Not just to her words, but to the spaces between them.

His presence was never hurried, never performative. He would sit with Nora, coaxing her gently into speech, easing her discomfort with warmth that didn't feel like charity.

And then there were the moments—quiet ones—when he would remain a while longer, speaking with Katherine about nothing of great consequence.

The price of coal. The direction of the wind. A book he'd read and found dull.

She found herself looking forward to these idle exchanges with a longing that made her feel foolish.

One afternoon, while Henry poured medicine into a small glass bottle, Katherine stood by the window, arms folded, eyes on the grey street below.

Liam was at Mary's, Nora asleep. The silence between them was not uncomfortable.

"You've been quieter lately," Henry remarked, sealing the stopper with a precise press.

Katherine turned her gaze to him, lips twitching into something like a smile.

"I've had much to think about."

He offered no reply, merely inclined his head. She wondered if he knew—if he sensed the dangerous path she had walked.

There were times when his eyes lingered on her face with the weight of unspoken understanding.

As he stood to leave, he paused beside the door, glancing back.

"I'm not in the habit of interfering in matters that aren't mine," he said, his voice lower than usual. "But should you ever find yourself in need of help—any kind of help—I hope you know you can ask."

Katherine's breath caught.

She nodded once, but the words she might have spoken stuck fast in her throat.

After he left, she stood there for a long while, one hand pressed against the cool glass, watching his figure retreat down the street.

IT WAS LATER that same week, beneath the smog-laced haze of evening, that Katherine saw something she wasn't meant to see.

She had finished work at the factory and, with the children safely at Mary's, had set out on a short errand for bread.

Her path took her through the southern end of the market square, near the rear of a tavern that Marcus frequented. She rarely passed this way—it had too many corners, too many eyes—but this time, a shortcut seemed worth the risk.

That was when she saw him.

Marcus, standing in the lee of the tavern wall, his voice low and measured as he spoke with two men dressed in the tailored coats of city officials.

One she recognised—Mr Fallon, a tax clerk known among the factory workers for his harsh levies and quieter indulgences. The other was less familiar, though his polished boots and confident stance spoke of authority.

Katherine stopped beneath the shadow of a butcher's awning, ducking behind a stack of empty crates.

The wind carried Marcus's voice only in snatches —something about "distribution" and "safe passage."

One of the officials handed Marcus a coin purse with a practised subtlety that betrayed long familiarity.

A coil of unease twisted in her stomach.

She'd long suspected Marcus's business extended beyond stolen trinkets and discreet smuggling. But this—this looked organised, deliberate. And it involved men who ought to be upholding the law.

She waited until the three parted ways, then slipped away unseen, her pulse thudding like a drumbeat behind her eyes.

That night, Katherine barely slept.

Even with Nora's steady breathing beside her, even with Liam nestled under her arm, the knowledge burrowed deeper.

Whatever Marcus was involved in, it was larger —and darker—than she had been led to believe.

. . .

THE NEXT DAY, she watched him carefully.

He came to the factory late in the afternoon, under the pretence of speaking with the owner, but she knew better now.

Marcus didn't glance at her, but that, too, seemed calculated—as if he were aware she might be watching.

Katherine went about her tasks with practised precision, her hands steady even as her thoughts churned.

If Marcus was colluding with officials, it meant the danger she faced wasn't merely criminal—it was systemic.

She couldn't count on the law to protect her if things went wrong.

And that changed everything.

AT SUPPER, as Mary stirred a pot of porridge for the children, Katherine sat by the fire, quiet.

Nora was well enough now to read scraps of old newsprint Mary had scavenged, and Liam played quietly with two wooden pegs he'd fashioned into soldiers.

The normalcy of the scene might have comforted her—had she not known what lay beneath it all.

Mary glanced over.

"You're brooding," she said plainly.

Katherine blinked. "Just tired."

Mary didn't push. She never did. But her knowing eyes rested on Katherine for a moment longer before she turned back to the pot.

LATER THAT EVENING, Henry arrived again.

He carried no satchel this time—just a wrapped parcel of apples and a tin of salve for Nora's chapped hands.

The children clamoured around him with easy affection, and Katherine stood aside, heart swollen with a mixture of warmth and guilt.

When the children had settled, and Henry stood to leave, she followed him to the doorway.

"I saw something," she said suddenly, her voice barely above a whisper.

He paused, turning back.

"I don't know what it means, not exactly," she continued. "But Marcus—he's involved with men who wear the city's crest. They're not just buyers. There's more to it."

Henry's expression tightened, but he said nothing.

"I've done things," Katherine added, voice rough. "To get medicine. For Nora. I don't regret that. But I won't be a pawn in something I don't understand."

He nodded slowly.

"I'm not surprised to hear that."

She looked at him.

"What should I do?"

"Trust your instinct," he said. "And be cautious. Very cautious."

And then, softer: "You're not alone in this."

THAT NIGHT, as the children slept and the boarding house creaked with the sound of old timbers settling, Katherine sat by the hearth with a single candle lit.

She thought of the roads that had brought her here—the desperation, the quiet hope, the ruthless choices.

She thought of Marcus's polished words, his veiled threats.

She thought of Henry's hands, firm and kind.

And she thought of her children, the way Liam curled into her side, the way Nora's laughter was slowly returning.

She would not let them be caught in a web spun by men who trafficked in secrets and fear.

The next morning, as the sky bloomed grey above the city, Katherine walked with purpose toward the part of town where Marcus kept his ledger.

She had a plan forming—half mad, half brave.

If she could find out what Marcus truly wanted… if she could discover what he was hiding behind his affable smiles and heavy coin purses… perhaps she could end this.

Not just for herself. But for everyone like her.

Women with no one to turn to.

Children who needed more than hope.

It was time to stop running.

It was time to find the truth.

CHAPTER 8

Katherine didn't plan to follow Marcus. It simply happened.

She had left the factory with the lingering dread of his earlier visit.

He had said little—only a quiet, "You know where to find me," murmured as he passed her by the workroom door.

But the way he said it, the steel behind his words dressed in silk, left her unnerved.

That afternoon, after seeing Henry's worried glance and feeling Mary's quiet scrutiny, Katherine knew she needed answers.

She could no longer rely on hope or instinct alone. She needed certainty.

And so, instead of returning straight home, she wrapped her shawl tighter and walked the long way through the city's narrowing lanes until she saw Marcus's familiar figure ahead, moving at a brisk pace toward the southern quarter.

She followed, careful not to let her footsteps echo too loudly on the damp stones.

What she saw chilled her to the bone.

He wasn't meeting fellow smugglers, as she'd first assumed.

No whispers in alleyways or furtive handovers.

Instead, he disappeared into a side entrance of the local constabulary.

Katherine stopped dead.

She pressed herself into the shadows, heart pounding.

She knew that building well—its barred windows, the heavy door with its peeling blue paint.

It was where the local police operated from.

Where frightened mothers reported missing children.

Where men were dragged by their collars after drunken brawls.

And Marcus Denton had walked in as if he belonged there.

She waited, half-convinced she'd imagined it.

But he emerged not ten minutes later, accompanied by a man she recognised only from whispered rumours—the station sergeant, a man said to be as corrupt as he was feared.

The two men shook hands like equals. No deference. No tension.

Katherine turned away before they could see her, her mind a storm.

Marcus was not simply a criminal—he was protected.

Tied, somehow, to the very men who were meant to uphold the law. And that meant any misstep she made wouldn't land her in gaol because she was unlucky—it would be deliberate. Orchestrated.

She was caught between two powers: the shadowed world of smuggling, and the cold machinery of the law. And both answered to Marcus Denton.

As she slipped away into the fog, her breath came in short, ragged bursts.

Every street now felt dangerous. Every glance from a passer-by was suspicious. The world had tilted sideways.

By the time she reached the boarding house, dusk was closing in. She climbed the stairs quietly, her thoughts louder than her steps.

Mary looked up as she entered their room.

"You're late," she said, gentle but firm.

Katherine managed a small nod.

"I lost track of time."

Mary studied her for a moment.

Then, softly, "Is it Denton?"

Katherine blinked.

"Why would you think that?"

"I'm not blind," Mary replied. "And I've heard things. I don't ask because I don't want to force you, but—if he's hurt you, or—"

"No," Katherine interrupted. "He hasn't touched me. But it's worse than I thought. He's not just part of this—he owns it. And the police... they're in his pocket."

Mary paled.

She crossed the room and lowered her voice to a whisper.

"You have to stop, Katherine. Whatever it is you've been doing—stop it."

"I can't," she replied. "Not yet. I'm in too deep. If I refuse, he could ruin me. And not just me—he knows about Nora. He used her illness as a hook."

Mary reached for her hand.

"Then let me help."

Katherine pulled away gently.

"I won't drag you into this. You've done enough already."

In truth, her fear now extended to anyone who knew her.

She didn't dare say too much to Henry either, though he was sharp enough to sense the danger.

She was a woman stitched into a web of silence, her lips sealed not by shame, but by strategy. Speaking could destroy those around her.

That night, as she sat by the fire and watched Liam drift into sleep, Katherine turned her thoughts to escape.

There had to be a way out.

But every possibility ended in peril. If she fled, Marcus would follow. If she confessed to Henry, he might try to intervene—and be hurt because of it. If she refused Marcus, the law itself could be turned against her.

She had nowhere to run.

And yet she could not stay where she was.

OVER THE NEXT FEW DAYS, Marcus was unusually silent. No notes. No visits. No requests. Katherine found the silence more terrifying than his presence.

It meant he was planning something.

And she didn't trust surprises.

Henry continued to visit, though less frequently, perhaps sensing her reticence.

Each time, he examined Nora with professional focus, but his eyes lingered on Katherine with something unspoken—worry, perhaps. Or suspicion.

"Your daughter's stronger," he said one evening, after checking Nora's pulse. "You should be proud."

"I'm just relieved," Katherine murmured.

He paused.

"If something's troubling you—something beyond Nora—I wish you'd tell me."

Katherine looked away.

"It's nothing."

Henry leaned forward.

"Katherine, I know what desperation looks like. And I've seen too much of it in your eyes lately."

"You see too much," she said, her voice sharper than intended.

But he didn't flinch.

"That may be. But I'd rather see too much than not enough."

She didn't answer.

When he left, Katherine felt the absence of his presence like a door closing.

. . .

IT WAS the following morning that Marcus returned.

He was waiting outside the boarding house, dressed impeccably in his usual dark coat, his boots gleaming.

Katherine's stomach turned the moment she saw him.

"Walk with me," he said.

She didn't dare refuse.

They strolled through the narrow lanes, his hand lightly resting on her elbow, a gesture that might seem gallant to any passer-by, but to Katherine felt like a shackle.

"You've done well," he said. "Reliable. Unobtrusive. That's hard to find."

She didn't reply.

"I have a delivery tomorrow night. Something a little more delicate than usual."

"What is it?" she asked cautiously.

He smiled.

"You know better than to ask that."

Her jaw clenched.

"But it's not just the usual," he continued. "It's time-sensitive. And it must reach its destination without fail. Think of it as a test."

"A test for what?"

He leaned close, his breath warm against her cheek.

"Your future."

There it was—the subtle threat wrapped in promise. Fail, and you're finished. Succeed, and the trap tightens.

When she returned home, Katherine stood in the middle of their room, trembling. The noose was drawing tighter. She could barely breathe.

She had to get out.

She had to do it *soon*.

THAT EVENING, Henry visited again. He noticed her pallor at once.

"Katherine," he said gently, "you're not well."

"I'm fine," she lied.

He sat across from her, his eyes searching.

"I saw Denton speaking with Sergeant Hawthorne last week."

She froze.

Henry nodded slowly.

"I thought it odd. Then I remembered the parcel you carried two weeks ago. The one you didn't think I saw you hide in your shawl."

Katherine's breath caught.

"I don't know what you're involved in," he said carefully, "but I suspect it's dangerous."

"I had no choice," she whispered.

"There's always a choice," he said. "It just doesn't always feel like it."

"I did it for Nora."

"I know."

He stood, stepping toward her, his tone low.

"If you want out, I'll help you. But I need to know everything."

Katherine's throat tightened. She felt the urge to unburden herself—every fear, every secret, every quiet cry in the night.

But she shook her head.

"Not yet."

Henry studied her.

Then, with a quiet nod, he said, "When you're ready."

THAT NIGHT, Katherine walked the streets long after the children were asleep. Her thoughts circled like hawks.

If she accepted the delivery, she was complicit in something darker than theft.

If she refused, Marcus would retaliate.

If she ran, she might be hunted.

But if she told Henry everything...

It wasn't just about trust. It was about protection.

She needed a way out that didn't end with her children in the streets or herself in a prison cell.

She passed the constabulary, its windows glowing dully. Men like Marcus didn't fear this place. They *used* it.

But maybe... maybe there were others who could still be trusted. Maybe Henry knew someone. A magistrate? A solicitor? Someone willing to hear the truth.

She didn't know.

But she *had* to find out.

THE NEXT MORNING, Marcus sent word. The delivery was to be made at midnight.

Katherine stared at the note, then burned it in the fire.

Her decision was made.

She would go to Henry.

Not just for herself—but for Mary. For Liam. For Nora.

For every woman walking that same tightrope between hunger and survival.

Because Marcus Denton's web was larger than her. But she would be the one to unpick the threads.

One by one.

CHAPTER 9

*K*atherine should have known better than to trust Marcus Denton.

He waited for her in the narrow courtyard behind the glassworks, the same place he had used before.

She'd come because she had no other choice—not truly.

Not with Nora still recovering, not with Liam so thin despite the broth and bread she scraped together.

She'd come wrapped in layers, the wind slicing through even the thickest of shawls, the weight of dread pressing heavier than the cold.

But tonight was different.

Marcus was waiting not with his usual polished

smile, but with something colder beneath the surface.

"You're early," he said.

"You didn't say I couldn't be," she replied.

He handed her a parcel—larger than usual, wrapped tightly and sealed with wax.

"This goes to Hampden Street. Number seventeen. You're to leave it in the alley entrance, under the stair. No knocking. No questions."

Katherine took it, surprised by how her hands didn't shake. She was getting used to the fear.

Marcus stepped closer, his voice low.

"And Katherine—if you think about double-crossing me, even for a moment, I'd advise against it."

"What are you talking about?"

His eyes narrowed.

"You've been asking questions. Watching. People have noticed."

Katherine stiffened.

"And what would you do about it, Marcus? Report me? To your friends at the constabulary?"

His smile was slow, poisonous.

"I wouldn't need to. They already know who you are."

Her mouth went dry.

"They know you've been making deliveries," he continued. "But they won't act—so long as you remain… useful."

There it was. The trap laid bare.

"You're working with them," she said, barely above a whisper.

He didn't deny it.

"Informant, courier, middleman—call me what you like. But it keeps me safe. And now it keeps you safe, too. So long as you do as you're told."

Katherine felt as though the cobbles beneath her shifted.

"You're not just part of this," she said. "You're managing it."

"That's right."

"And you've been using me."

He leaned in again.

"Every move you've made since the day I caught you at the apothecary? It's been mine. And if you ever want to see your daughter grow up, you'll remember that."

For a moment, she saw herself striking him— hard, without thinking—but she didn't. She turned, parcel clutched against her chest, and walked away.

Not because she was afraid.

But because she needed to survive long enough to destroy him.

She didn't go straight to Hampden Street.

Instead, she walked the long route home, mind racing. Marcus's admission confirmed everything she had begun to suspect. He was no common smuggler. He was embedded in the very system meant to stop men like him.

And worse—she was now officially in his debt, in his web, his leverage.

Back in her small room, the children already asleep, Katherine sat on the floor near the fire, parcel beside her.

She hadn't told Henry.

She'd stopped short of confession more than once, afraid he might try to fix something that couldn't be mended.

He'd been kind to her. Too kind. And in some ways, that was worse than cruelty. It made her feel seen.

She heard his words from earlier that week, ringing in her mind.

"There's always a choice. It just doesn't always feel like it."

But what choice did she have now?

The next morning, Henry came by again—just

before dawn.

Nora was resting, and Liam was still asleep. Katherine stood at the hearth, hands wrapped around a chipped mug of tea.

"You didn't come yesterday," Henry said quietly.

"I was working," she replied.

He studied her.

"You look like you haven't slept."

She didn't answer.

"Is it Denton?"

The question hung in the air like smoke.

Katherine stared into her tea.

"He's not who I thought he was."

"Then tell me who he is."

But she couldn't—not completely.

"I don't want you involved," she said.

"I already am," Henry replied, voice firm. "You brought your daughter to me. You trusted me to help her. That means something."

"I didn't want to trust you," she whispered. "But I had no choice."

He stepped closer.

"Then let me give you one now."

She looked up, eyes meeting his. Something in her cracked, but only a little.

"I can't," she said, and her voice broke on the word. "Not yet."

Henry nodded once, disappointment carefully hidden.

"When you can," he said, and left without another word.

THAT EVENING, she made the delivery.

She left the parcel under the stair at number seventeen Hampden Street, exactly as instructed, then turned and walked back into the dark, hands clenched so tightly her palms throbbed.

She thought it would get easier.

It didn't.

But she had made a decision. Not to stop—not yet. But to endure, to watch, to learn.

And when the moment came, she would be ready.

The next day, Henry returned. He didn't ask about Denton.

Instead, he sat beside Nora and read from a book he had brought, his voice steady and warm. Katherine sat nearby, watching them both, something heavy and unspoken settling between her ribs.

After Nora fell asleep, Henry turned to her.

"Something's coming," he said. "You feel it too, don't you?"

Katherine nodded.

"When it does—don't face it alone."

She didn't answer. But she remembered the words.

THAT NIGHT, Marcus sent word again.

Another delivery. Another test.

This time, Katherine didn't reply.

Instead, she went to Mary.

"I need to tell you something," she said.

Mary listened—quiet, still—while Katherine told her everything. Not every name, not every detail. But enough.

Mary didn't interrupt.

When she was done, her friend reached across the table and took her hand.

"You did what you had to."

"I betrayed myself."

"No," Mary said. "You survived."

Tears sprang in Katherine's eyes, unbidden and unwelcome.

"I'm going to get out," she whispered. "I just don't know how yet."

"Then we'll find a way. Together."

Later that night, after the children were in bed, Katherine sat by the fire and stared at the flickering flames.

She had sworn to protect them—to do whatever was necessary. She had carried parcels, accepted blood money, lied to kind men.

But she would not let it break her.

She would be smart. She would be patient.

And when the time came, she would be the one to end it.

She closed her eyes and made the vow again, silently.

For Nora. For Liam. For herself.

Whatever it cost.

She would find the way out.

And when she did, Marcus Denton would regret ever thinking she was his pawn.

CHAPTER 10

*T*he door to the alley swung shut behind her, and Katherine felt the cold settle into her bones.

She hadn't meant to linger so long after the delivery, but Marcus had kept her waiting, spinning one of his silken threats into a low, amused tone that made her skin crawl.

"You're cleverer than the others," he'd said as he handed over the parcel. "That's why you'll do this one—and the next. You're not foolish enough to think you're free of me yet."

His voice still echoed in her mind as she stepped into the fog-drenched street, the weight of the coins in her pocket doing little to steady her.

They should have brought relief. Instead, they

pressed against her like stones tied to the hem of a drowning woman's skirt.

When she reached the lodging house, she found Mary sitting outside her room, arms folded tightly, face tight with worry.

"He came by," Mary said without preamble. "Tall man. The one with the smooth voice."

Katherine's breath caught.

"He didn't say much. Just looked around, said he'd return. But it wasn't friendly, Katherine. It felt… like a warning."

"I'm sorry," Katherine whispered, her voice thin. "He's trying to trap me."

Mary's eyes softened, though the concern didn't leave her face.

"I don't want to know what you're caught up in—not if it puts me or the children at risk. But you should know, I'll stand by you. Just… tell me the truth when it matters."

Katherine nodded, the weight of gratitude almost too much to bear.

That night, she sat by the fire with Nora nestled close and Liam asleep against her side. The children were better—stronger, laughing more, eating more.

Henry's visits had helped, not only with medicine

but with kindness. It was that kindness that unsettled her most.

She'd begun to anticipate the soft knock at the door in the evenings, the way he'd tip his hat and step inside, always with some small offering. Apples. A roll of bandage. A worn book for Liam.

He spoke to her gently, never prying, though his eyes held questions. And in the stillness between the children's breathing and the low hiss of the fire, she'd begun to see what her life might have looked like—if things had been different.

But it wasn't different.

And it was Marcus who knew the truth about her.

Not Henry.

Not Mary.

And it was Marcus who had come today with a different kind of threat.

He hadn't just spoken of deliveries this time. He'd named her children.

"Nora's looking brighter," he'd said casually. "That little cough's gone now, hasn't it? You've done well. Be a shame if she caught another chill."

The implication was clear. Every kindness Marcus had shown was a chain. Every coin she took bound her more tightly to him.

And now he wanted more.

KATHERINE THOUGHT of the tall stranger that Mary had spoken about.

She hadn't needed to ask her anything more about him.

She knew exactly who he was and her blood had felt like it had frozen in her veins.

She'd hoped that he wouldn't come again, but that had been wishful thinking because just a few days later, as if he'd been watching for her, he stepped out of a dark corner, as if he was made of the shadows themselves and had brought her to an abrupt halt.

Her breathing had become erratic just at the sight of him.

He hadn't even bothered with the barest of salutations, he'd got straight to the point.

"You'll find a way to bring me word of Denton's dealings," he'd said, his voice quiet but firm. "Whatever he's planning, whoever he speaks to—you pass it on. Quietly. Or I speak to the wrong people and your little family disappears."

The rage that bloomed in Katherine's chest was

almost blinding. But she'd said nothing. Only nodded.

Because she knew Ned Riley too well.

ONCE, long ago, back in Ireland, she had feared no man more. He had run the docks with a brutality that chilled the bones.

There had been whispers of what he'd done to women who crossed him—or merely looked the wrong way. And now he stood before her again, not as some ghost of the past, but as a real and present danger.

Alive. Watching. Hunting.

The very man that she had run away from.

"I want a cut," he'd added. "Whatever Denton's paying you, half comes to me. That's the price for my silence."

And that, more than anything else, made her feel sick.

Because Ned Riley never stopped at half.

THE NEXT MORNING, Katherine moved with care, feeling the weight of both men pressing in on her.

She hadn't slept. Had barely eaten. Her thoughts felt fractured, her breath thin.

At the factory, her fingers slipped more than once on the tiny metal clasps, earning a sharp word from the overseer. Mary kept casting glances her way, but Katherine didn't meet them.

It wasn't until the midday break that she found a moment to speak.

"I need to ask something of you," Katherine said quietly as they sat on the back step, steam from their tea rising into the grey air. "If something were to happen—if I disappeared—would you take the children?"

Mary's eyes widened.

"Don't say things like that."

"I mean it."

"No," Mary said firmly. "Don't talk like you're already lost."

But Katherine only looked down at her tea, her hands trembling around the tin cup.

THAT EVENING, Henry arrived again, carrying a wrapped bundle of herbs and a bag of barley.

"From the market," he said. "It's not much, but I thought it might stretch a stew."

Katherine took it with a small smile, guilt rising in her throat.

"You're too kind," she said, not quite meeting his gaze.

He paused.

"Katherine… I know something's wrong. And I don't want to pry. But I'd rather you spoke now than have to find out later from someone in uniform."

She closed her eyes.

"What if I told you I've made mistakes?"

"I'd say we all do."

"What if I told you I've put my children in danger?"

"I'd ask how I could help."

That broke her.

The tears came quietly, unannounced. She turned away, but he stepped closer, a warm hand on her shoulder.

"I'm not asking you to explain it all," Henry said. "Not yet. But please… trust me enough to let me help you. Whatever this is—it's bigger than you."

Katherine drew a shaky breath.

"There's a man from my past. He's found me. And now he's forcing me to spy. On Marcus. He knows I've been doing work for him."

Henry's jaw tightened.

"You've been smuggling for Denton?"

"For the medicine. For Nora. It was the only way. But now Ned Riley wants his share, and if I refuse— he'll hurt my children. Or worse."

Henry didn't speak for a long moment.

Then he said,

"We'll find a way out."

"There is no way out," she whispered.

"There's always a way," he said. "But you can't face it alone."

By the following evening, Katherine had made a decision.

She would pretend to play Ned's game—but use it to buy time.

Let him believe she would spy on Marcus. Let Marcus believe she remained loyal. Let Henry begin to find a solution.

She would survive this. Not just for herself, but for her children.

When she saw Ned that night, she kept her face carefully neutral.

"I've asked about Denton," she said. "He's moving something big next week. Details aren't clear."

Ned grunted, satisfied for now. He tossed her a few shillings, the gesture almost lazy.

"That's better," he said. "See? You're useful. Keep it up."

She turned away, her hands clenched tight in her coat.

Behind her, Ned called,

"Tell him you want more. That'll make him talk."

But Katherine didn't reply.

She walked into the dark, wind cutting through her like a blade, and promised herself she would see this through.

Even if it meant walking the edge of a knife.

CHAPTER 11

*K*atherine's fingers trembled as she slid the last sheet of parchment back into the ledger. The room smelt of coal dust and cold ink, the back office dim despite the morning sun filtering weakly through the high, grimy window.

She had crept into Marcus Denton's private study during his absence, each second ticking louder in her mind than the last. Her heart thudded so violently she feared it might echo through the thin walls of the warehouse.

She had come under the pretence of delivering a small satchel of trinkets for cataloguing—a request Marcus had sent by note the night before.

He was due back shortly, and Katherine knew

she had no more than minutes before a clerk or courier might appear to fetch her.

But what she had found among his papers had chilled her to the bone.

It wasn't merely records of contraband or routes through the city.

There were names—officials, constables, city clerks—all neatly aligned with payments, drops, favours.

Denton's empire reached far beyond the alley shadows and stolen parcels. He operated in the daylight too, with men who wore the law like armour.

She folded the page carefully, sliding it into the seam of her glove. A risk. A heavy one. But she needed proof—something beyond whispers and suspicion. If Denton ever turned on her, she needed more than her word.

The moment she stepped from the study, she nearly collided with one of Denton's errand boys. She smiled, made some flustered excuse, and hurried back into the city, the echo of her footfalls betraying the shaking in her limbs.

.   .   .

HENRY WATCHED her closely that evening. He said nothing of her pale complexion or the way her hands shook slightly when she poured tea, but Katherine felt the weight of his gaze like a pressing hand on her shoulder.

"You've not been sleeping again," he said finally.

She offered him a weary smile.

"There's not been time for sleep."

"You're wearing yourself thin."

Katherine looked away, fingers tightening around her teacup.

She hated this—this tenderness.

Not because it was unwelcome, but because it unravelled her resolve. Henry had become a source of calm, but also a mirror. When he looked at her, he saw things she hadn't meant to reveal.

"I'm managing," she said softly. "Nora is stronger. That's all that matters."

Henry set down his cup.

"Is it? Because lately, it seems you're slipping further into something that has little to do with your daughter."

Katherine froze.

"I've never pried, Katherine. I've tried to give you space. But every time I see you, you look more like someone trying not to drown."

The words cut deeper than he knew.

"Henry, please—"

"Just tell me you're not in danger."

She opened her mouth, but nothing came. Because how could she lie to him now?

"Would it matter if I were?" she asked finally, voice brittle.

Henry stood and crossed the small room, crouching beside her. His hand found hers and held it gently.

"It matters to me."

Tears pricked her eyes, but she blinked them away.

"I can't talk about it. Not yet."

He nodded once.

"Then I'll wait. But when you're ready, Katherine, I'll be here."

TWO DAYS LATER, Denton tested her again.

He had summoned her to a warehouse along the river—a new location, unfamiliar and exposed. She knew immediately it was a test.

The package he gave her was heavy, wrapped in oilcloth, and the address scrawled on the note he handed over meant crossing the heart of the city—

where constables watched street corners with idle menace.

"I need to know I can count on you," he said lightly, but his eyes pinned her like a blade.

Katherine nodded, feigning calm.

But she knew this delivery wasn't about cargo—it was about control. Denton suspected her. She could feel it in the way his eyes lingered on her gloves, the slight pause when he passed her the parcel.

She carried it with her heart in her throat, every breath tight in her chest.

Twice she thought she was being followed—once by a boy who turned down an alley before she could be sure, and once by a tall man in a constable's coat, who never once looked her way but whose presence rang warning bells in her mind.

When she reached the destination, a boarding house near the docks, she handed over the parcel to a man who did not speak, did not even meet her eyes. It was done.

But the damage had been done too. Denton's silence over the next few days was louder than any words.

HENRY NOTICED the change in her.

"You're barely eating," he said one evening, after Mary had taken Liam and Nora to fetch more coal.

"There's too much to do," Katherine replied, voice thin.

"And too much you're not telling me."

He waited. When she didn't respond, he stepped closer, lowering his voice.

"I know Denton's involved in more than you say. I've heard whispers in the market, from men who've treated bruises he left behind. If you're caught in his net—"

"I'm trying to get out," Katherine interrupted, her voice cracking.

Henry stilled.

"I didn't mean for any of this," she whispered. "I only wanted to help Nora. It was supposed to be once, just once."

"And now?"

"Now I don't know how to stop."

Henry's expression softened.

"Then let me help you."

Katherine hesitated. Then, slowly, she pulled the folded ledger page from her glove and handed it to him.

"I took this from his office."

Henry read it once, then again.

"This… this could bury him."

"Or me, if he realises it's missing."

He folded the page carefully.

"We'll go to the magistrate. A trusted one. I have a friend—he's not like the rest."

"Are you sure?"

"As sure as I can be."

But before they could act, another storm broke.

It was Ned.

Katherine had almost forgotten about him—her tormentor from Ireland, the reason she'd fled. But now he was in London.

Since his first threats she'd barely seen him.

She done her best to stay out of his way but it would seem that was no longer going to be allowed. It seemed he was determined to make sure that she stuck with the deal that he'd made her agree to.

After a few weeks of no contact she imagined that she could feel his eyes upon her as she walked to and from the button factory, though she never saw him.

She saw him first from across the street, stepping out of a tavern as she passed with Liam. Her blood ran cold. His eyes found hers instantly. The smile he gave was slow. Measured.

He followed her the next day. Said nothing. Just lingered.

Then, one evening, she found a scrap of paper pinned to the door of her room.

"Still think you can run, girl?"

It was a another stark reminder that he still wanted information on Marcus.

Katherine nearly fell to her knees.

She told Mary everything. The tears came then— helpless, exhausted. Mary held her, said nothing until the shaking passed.

"You'll not face him alone," Mary said. "Not this time."

Katherine shook her head. "He knows where we live."

"Then we'll move. We'll hide. You've friends here now, Katherine. You're not the woman who ran with nothing."

BUT THE TERROR REMAINED.

Katherine barely slept.

She walked Nora to the doctor herself, kept Liam

by her side at all times. She was waiting for the blow to fall—whether from Marcus, or Ned, or the law.

The only thing that gave her hope was the paper Henry had hidden away, the promise of justice. But it felt too fragile. Too late.

A WEEK PASSED. Then another.

Marcus called again—this time less friendly.

"You've been distant," he said.

"I've had a sick child."

"You're not as clever as you think," he replied. "I'll find out what you've done."

That night, her window was broken. Nothing stolen. Just a warning.

She went to Henry the next morning.

"Now," she said. "We go now."

THE MAGISTRATE HENRY took her to was grey-haired and sharp-eyed. He said little, but asked hard questions. Katherine answered them all.

When she handed over the ledger page, he studied it carefully.

"This alone is not enough," he said. "But it's a beginning."

"A beginning?" Katherine echoed. "I need protection. For my children."

"You'll have it. But tread carefully. Denton has friends. We'll build a case. Quietly. Then bring it all down at once."

She left with a mix of dread and hope. It was the first time she had felt anything like agency since arriving in London.

THAT NIGHT, she sat beside Nora's bed. Liam slept beside them, his curls a soft tangle against the blanket.

Henry had promised she was safe. The magistrate had promised action.

But she knew better than to believe in safety.

Not yet.

Not while Marcus Denton still walked free.

Not while Ned still lingered in the shadows.

She had started this to save her daughter.

Now, she had to finish it to save them all.

CHAPTER 12

*T*he Crystal Palace loomed ahead like a cathedral of light, its vast iron ribs shimmering beneath the gaslit sky.

Katherine stood just outside its grand entrance, the chatter of London's elite curling through the winter air like perfume. She adjusted her shawl and smoothed the front of her borrowed gown, the unfamiliar satin whispering with every breath she took.

She did not belong here.

The knowledge was a stone in her gut. Around her, women glided in silks and feathers, men laughed in velvet waistcoats, and trays of wine glinted like jewels on silver platters. Yet here she was, amidst them, slipping through the crowd not as a guest, but as a spy.

Marcus Denton was somewhere inside.

Katherine's fingers tightened around the small clutch in her hand. Hidden inside was a folded note from one of Mary's contacts: *Denton. Crystal Palace. 7. Watch him.*

It had been scrawled hastily, but it was all she needed. Whatever Marcus was orchestrating now, it was important. Important enough to draw the highest of society into the trap.

As she passed beneath the arched glass entrance, a steward barely glanced at her forged invitation. The grandeur inside stole her breath: palms in bronze pots, chandeliers dripping with crystal, the murmur of music floating from the far ballroom. Every surface gleamed. Katherine had never seen such decadence.

Her boots, well-polished but humble, felt louder than gunshots on the marble floor.

She moved carefully, scanning the sea of faces. Marcus wouldn't appear too early, not when he preferred to make an entrance. So she watched. Waited. Pretended. Her lips held a neutral smile as she wandered from one ornate chamber to another, each more gilded than the last.

She paused beside a table of pastries she couldn't name, the smell of sugar and almonds making her stomach twist. It had been days since she'd eaten anything more than broth and bread. But hunger was not why she was here.

When Marcus arrived, she felt it before she saw him.

A hush rippled. Heads turned. He strode in wearing a tailcoat so perfectly tailored it could've been sewn to his skin. His dark hair was slicked back, his smile easy, his manner casual. He belonged here.

Unlike her.

Katherine took a step back, placing herself partially behind a potted fern. From here, she could observe him unnoticed. He greeted people with that same smooth charm, laughed with a baroness, kissed the hand of a foreign ambassador's wife. It was all theatre. But she had seen behind the curtain.

He wasn't just charming. He was dangerous.

She followed him at a distance as he moved between conversations, slowly weaving toward a quieter gallery. There, flanked by velvet drapes and lesser-known aristocrats, he began to speak in hushed tones with two older gentlemen.

Katherine edged closer, careful to stay near the columns. The murmur of violins from the ballroom cloaked her movements.

"They don't know," one man was saying. "The documents are still secure."

Marcus's voice was quieter.

"They'd best remain so. If word leaks, it's not just reputations that fall."

"You're certain about the girl?"

A chill swept Katherine's spine. They didn't mean her. They couldn't.

"She's... useful," Marcus said. "For now. But if she becomes a problem, you'll hear no protest from me."

Katherine's stomach flipped.

He *knew*. Or at least suspected.

She backed away slowly, nearly colliding with a maid balancing a tray of champagne. The woman frowned but said nothing.

She had to leave. Now.

She turned toward the ballroom, planning her exit, when a familiar face emerged from the crowd.

Henry.

He wore a suit she had never seen, simple but well-fitted, and his eyes searched the crowd until they found hers. Relief and worry warred in his expression. He moved quickly to her side.

"What are you doing here?" he asked in a low voice.

"Watching," she whispered. "Marcus is deeper in

this than we thought. He's speaking to men who talk of *documents* and *falling reputations*. And he mentioned a girl. I think he means me."

Henry paled.

"Then we must go. Now."

But it was too late.

From across the room, Marcus's eyes found hers. His smile didn't falter, but the temperature seemed to drop around them. He inclined his head politely and turned back to his companions, but she saw it. The tightening of his jaw. The flicker of calculation.

He knew she was here. He knew she'd heard.

Katherine felt Henry take her elbow.

"We'll exit through the east corridor. Follow me."

They moved swiftly but calmly, navigating the fringes of the party, down a hallway lined with marble busts. As they passed a mirrored alcove, Katherine glanced over her shoulder.

Men were following.

Not in uniform. Not overt. But they were moving with intent, eyes fixed.

She didn't speak—only quickened her steps.

They emerged into a quiet courtyard, frost glinting on the hedges. Henry nodded to a gate near the servants' quarters.

"Through there. Hurry."

They slipped through just as a voice called out behind them. A man shouted. Katherine ran.

They didn't stop until they were deep into the side streets, the sounds of the Crystal Palace nothing but distant echoes.

Only then did Katherine allow herself to breathe.

Henry stopped, turning to face her.

"You're lucky. That could've ended very differently."

She nodded, chest heaving.

"But now we know. Marcus isn't just a smuggler. He's entrenched in something political. Dangerous."

Henry's brow furrowed.

"We'll need proof."

Katherine nodded, her expression hardening.

"Then we find it. Before he finds me."

FROM SOMEWHERE DEEP in the shadows, a figure watched them disappear into the fog.

Marcus Denton lit a cigarette and smiled.

"So," he murmured, "the mouse bites back."

But next time, he promised himself, he'd be ready.

CHAPTER 13

*K*atherine thought back to her secret search of Marcus Denton's study. She'd been looking for something that she might use against him – something that might give her knowledge and with that power.

She had no idea what that might be and so the information that she'd found had shocked her to the core.

But there it was, the papers that she'd found had confirmed it—sealed letters, tucked within a drawer of Marcus Denton's desk, bearing the wax crest of Lord Montclair himself.

There were more, of course—ledgers, coded messages, a carefully preserved birth certificate folded between pages of a Latin text. But it was the signature, the unmistakable flourish of Montclair's hand at the bottom of one page, that set Katherine's heart thudding like a trapped bird in her chest.

Marcus Denton was not just a smuggler with polished boots and venom on his tongue.

He was Montclair's bastard—abandoned, denied, left to rot among London's filth while his father dined with dukes.

And now, he meant to burn down the house that cast him out.

She had folded the page carefully, slid it into the seam of her glove. A risk. A dangerous one. But she had needed proof—something beyond whispers and suspicion. If Denton ever turned on her, she needed more than her word.

The moment she'd stepped from the study, she nearly collided with one of Marcus's errand boys and she thought that she'd been found out, but she'd smiled, made some flustered excuse, and hurried back into the city, the echo of her footfalls betraying the shaking in her limbs.

She hadn't run, though every instinct screamed for it.

· · ·

WHEN SHE'D NEXT SEEN Henry later that day, he'd known straight away that something had changed.

"You're hiding something," he had said gently, as they sat by the hearth with the children playing quietly nearby. "And I don't mean the fatigue."

Katherine sighed the fear of what she'd found gripping her.

"If I tell you, you'll try to fix it. But it can't be fixed."

"Try me."

She hesitated.

Then, in a low voice, she said, "Marcus Denton is Lord Montclair's son. Illegitimate. He's been hiding it, but I took proof."

And it was that proof that Katherine had hidden away, that proof that she'd held tight to her chest until Henry had suggested that they speak to his magistrate friend.

BUT SINCE THEN, she'd allowed herself to become more bold and she had once again taken herself into Marcus Denton's study wondering if there was more that she might be able to find. More information that might be able to bring about her freedom from him.

．　．　．

AND EVENTUALLY SHE thought that she may have found just that.

KATHERINE AND HENRY were discussing once again Marcus Denton's illegitimate birth and the document that she'd found to prove it.

"That's... significant. It explains his reach. His money." Henry said

"And his rage," Katherine murmured. "He's not just smuggling trinkets, Henry. He's planning something. Something political. Dangerous."

Henry was silent for a moment, then said, "You shouldn't be near him."

"I don't have a choice."

"You always have a choice."

Katherine stood abruptly, walked to the window. Fog clung to the panes.

"You think I haven't looked for one? I've begged for it. Bargained. Endured."

Henry rose too, gentler now. "Then let me help you. Please."

She turned—and the words spilled out before she could stop them.

"I've been carrying for him. Delivering things. Watching people. Because if I don't, he'll take it out on the children."

Henry's breath left him in a rush.

"Dear God."

"I thought I could keep control. That I could stay ahead of it. But he's watching me now. Testing me. He knows I'm not loyal."

She wrapped her arms around herself, as if to hold together what was splintering inside.

"I'm so tired, Henry. I can't sleep. I can't eat. I lie awake listening for footsteps on the stairs. Waiting for him to come and drag me out. Or worse."

Henry crossed the room in two strides. He took her hands in his, firm and warm.

"You're not alone. Not anymore."

And that was the moment the dam broke.

Katherine pressed her face to his chest, the sobs coming in ragged waves, too long suppressed. She felt his arms tighten around her, heard his voice murmuring comforts she couldn't quite grasp.

They stood that way for a long time, the fire casting soft shadows over the room, the children oblivious in their own little world.

When she could breathe again, she whispered,

"I'm sorry."

"For what?"

"For bringing this to your door. For the mess I've made."

Henry drew back just enough to meet her eyes.

"Don't be sorry for surviving. Don't be sorry for protecting your children. You did what you had to."

"I betrayed myself," she said quietly.

"No," he said. "You endured. And now… now we fight back."

A silence settled between them, taut with unspoken emotion.

Then Katherine said, "There's one more thing."

Henry's brow lifted slightly. "Yes?"

She reached into her glove and withdrew the folded page—the one with Montclair's crest, the one that could undo everything Denton had built.

"He's going to use this. I don't know how yet. But it's part of something bigger."

Henry took the paper, read it, his face unreadable.

When he looked back at her, something had shifted. Not just concern. Resolve.

"Then we stop him. But not with whispers. With proof. With names. And with allies who'll listen."

Katherine nodded, though fear still twisted in her gut. "He'll come for me if he knows I took it."

"Then we stay ahead of him."

And somehow, despite the looming storm, Katherine felt a flicker of hope. Fragile, yes. But real.

LATER THAT NIGHT, after Henry had gone and the children had been tucked safely into bed, Katherine sat by the fire with the note in her lap and the weight of everything pressing in.

She had begun this journey alone—desperate, frightened, and willing to barter anything for a vial of medicine.

Now she had something more dangerous than desperation.

She had purpose.

And if Denton meant to burn the world to reach his father, she would be standing in the ashes to make sure he failed.

One way or another.

CHAPTER 14

The candle guttered low as Katherine sat in the corner of the room, her hands clenched in her lap. The fire had long since burned down to embers, and still she hadn't moved. The children were asleep—Nora curled beneath a threadbare blanket, Liam's small form tucked against the wall—but Katherine's mind was ablaze.

The knock, when it came, was sharp. Controlled. Not Henry. Not Mary.

She opened the door a fraction and found Marcus Denton standing in the corridor, his silhouette neat and impeccable against the glow of the stairwell.

"May I come in?" he asked, as if he were a neighbour come to borrow tea.

She stepped aside without speaking.

He crossed the room slowly, his eyes flicking to the children, the empty hearth, the silence. Then he turned to her.

"There was a time," he said mildly, "when you would've met me in the courtyard. A time when you didn't make me chase shadows through city streets."

"I've had a sick child," she replied evenly. "You noticed."

A small smile tugged at the corner of his mouth. "That I did."

He removed his gloves, placed them on the table.

"Let's not waste time, Katherine. You've been asking questions. Following me. Listening where you shouldn't. And yet, here you are. Still useful. Still intact."

Katherine said nothing.

Marcus stepped closer, his voice softening.

"I want to tell you something. Something I've never said aloud—not to anyone."

She frowned. "Why?"

"Because understanding has value." He took a breath, then continued. "I was born in a servant's room at Montclair House. My mother—nothing more than a maid. My father, the master. A man who never acknowledged me. Who paid for silence but not dignity. When I was ten, she was turned out. I followed her into the streets. We starved. She died. I did not."

His voice didn't waver, but Katherine saw the gleam in his eyes. Not tears—no. Fury.

"I survived on scraps. Learned to steal. Learned to charm. And when the time came, I learned how to destroy the kind of men who had forgotten I existed. One by one."

He turned to her now, eyes bright. "This city bows to power. And I've built mine. Brick by brick. You see smuggling. I see strategy. You see corruption. I see leverage."

Katherine's breath caught. "You're trying to justify—"

"I'm showing you the truth. You and I aren't so different, Katherine. We both come from nothing. And we both want more—for ourselves, and for those we protect. You've lied. Stolen. Deceived. Tell me—was it not for them?" He nodded at the sleeping children.

"Yes," she said softly. "But I didn't make others suffer for it."

He studied her for a moment. "You think you're still above the mud you walk in. You're not."

Then his voice dropped. "Here is what happens

next. You stop digging. You stop watching. You become what I tell you to be—loyal. Or I undo you entirely."

She stiffened. "You won't harm them."

He smiled again, but this time there was no charm in it. "I don't make threats, Katherine. I set terms."

He stepped forward, his breath warm and sour. "Deliver something for me. One final time. And then we'll see how useful you can be."

He turned to leave, then paused. "Loyalty, Katherine. Or ruin. That is your choice."

The door closed behind him.

She stood motionless for a full minute before her knees buckled, and she sat heavily by the fire, breath ragged.

Loyalty—or ruin.

But it wasn't a choice. It was a noose.

SHE MET Henry the next morning beneath the old iron bridge, where the fog clung like old wool to the water's edge.

"I have to tell you something," she said, not waiting for pleasantries.

His brows drew together as she pulled a folded note from her coat.

"He gave me another task," she said. "But this time he told me why he does it. What he's built. How far it reaches."

Henry read the paper in silence. Then: "He confessed?"

"Not everything. But enough. Enough to understand him."

She looked out across the grey river.

"He's trapped, Henry. Just like me. All his power, and he's still that boy—starving, shamed, forgotten. Every scheme, every blackmail, every coin he squeezes from the city is revenge."

Henry said nothing, only placed a hand gently on her arm.

"I pity him," she murmured. "But I'm still going to stop him."

LATER THAT DAY, she found Ned waiting in the alley behind the baker's. His eyes were bloodshot, his breath stinking of gin and old rage.

"You've been slow," he growled.

"I've spoken to Denton," she said calmly. "He's

planning something. A new shipment. Arms. I don't know who for yet."

He grinned. "Knew you'd see sense."

"Don't mistake caution for obedience," she snapped.

His smile vanished. He stepped closer. "You think this is a game?"

"No. I think it's war."

He grabbed her wrist, hard enough to bruise. "You play both sides, girl, you burn on both ends. You forget what I am."

She stared at him, cold. "No. I remember exactly what you are."

He released her with a shove. "Next time, bring names. Or I start naming them myself."

THAT NIGHT, Katherine sat at the window long after the lamps were extinguished, watching the fog shift and scatter under moonlight.

She saw them now—Marcus and Ned.

Men born of violence. One masked in civility, the other in brute force. And in different ways, each of them imprisoned by what made them.

And herself? She had let them corner her, force her into silence, into complicity.

But that would end now.

No more waiting. No more pretending.

She would use what Marcus had given her—his secrets, his history, his carelessness. And she would use what Ned had forgotten—that she was no longer the girl who'd fled with nothing.

She was a mother.

And mothers fought.

THREE DAYS LATER, she met Marcus again.

He summoned her to the bookshop—a back room walled with ledgers and smoke-stained shelves.

"This is the delivery," he said, placing a leather case on the table. "You'll take it to the cellar beneath Ashton's Warehouse. Midnight. No deviation."

Katherine nodded.

Then, softly: "Marcus."

He looked up.

"I know who you are. What your father did. What you endured."

His mouth twitched. "Is this pity?"

"No. It's recognition. You wanted to shape the world into something that wouldn't spit on you. I understand that."

A long pause stretched.

"But I won't help you anymore," she added.

His expression hardened. "You think you can walk away?"

"No," she said. "I think I can burn the web."

She turned and left before he could reply.

SHE DID NOT GO to Ashton's Warehouse that night.

Instead, she met Henry behind the magistrate's office, the case clutched in gloved hands.

"It's here," she whispered. "Whatever's inside, it's enough to trigger a purge or a war."

Henry took it carefully.

"Are you sure?"

"No. But I'm ready."

He pressed a small paper into her palm.

"Names. A route out. If things go wrong."

She tucked it into her bodice.

Then she smiled.

"We double-cross them both."

THE NEXT EVENING, Ned was waiting.

"Where's the update?" he snapped.

She stepped into the alley, voice flat. "There is none."

"You what?"

"I'm done."

He advanced, rage bright. "You don't get to choose, girl."

But she was faster.

She stepped aside as Henry emerged from the shadows, two constables close behind.

"You were right," Katherine said, breath tight. "He never stops at half."

Ned swore and lunged—but the constables closed in. One twisted his arm behind his back, the other shoved him to the ground.

Henry turned to Katherine. "Now Denton."

MARCUS'S OFFICE was dark when they arrived, but not empty.

He stood behind the desk, hands clasped. "I thought you might come."

Katherine stepped forward, heart steady. "The game's over."

He laughed once—bitter, sharp. "You've no idea what's begun."

"The magistrate has what he needs. Documents. Names. Even the weapons route."

His smile faded.

"You were always clever," he murmured. "But you'll never be safe."

"Neither will you."

For a long moment, they stood facing each other.

Then Marcus said quietly, "Tell Nora I'm glad she's better."

It was the closest he would come to surrender.

BACK IN THEIR room that night, Katherine watched her children sleep.

The danger wasn't gone. Not truly. But it had changed shape—no longer the constant, pressing weight, but a shadow she had dragged into the light.

She thought of Marcus—his haunted eyes, his confession. She thought of Ned—snarling as he was taken. And she thought of herself, not as a pawn, but as a blade.

It was not over.

But it had begun to end.

CHAPTER 15

Katherine knew the hour had come to shift from survival to strategy. No more drifting on the tide of desperation. No more waiting for the next demand, the next knock, the next threat. If she wanted to protect Nora and Liam, if she wanted any kind of life beyond this cramped room and the fear that clung to its walls, she needed to act. Not react.

She began that morning as she always did—rising before dawn, checking on the children, fixing tea with water heated over the small fire. But her thoughts were not on the chores or the factory or what Mary might cook for supper. Her mind was with Marcus Denton.

Not the man she saw, all polished boots and

practised charm, but the man she now understood him to be. Ruthless. Untouchable. Backed by crooked constables and a network that slithered through every shadowed alley of the city. And yet, he had a vulnerability. One he couldn't bury beneath coin or charm: his name.

The Montclair name—his birthright denied, his shame cloaked in secrecy. The same secret he had hinted at when trying to impress her once.

"My bloodline is more noble than most would guess," he had murmured, his eyes glittering. "But titles aren't everything."

At the time, she had thought little of it. Now, she understood its weight.

He'd once called Lord Montclair "the old bastard." It was more than a turn of phrase. Marcus was illegitimate—unacknowledged, cast off. And bitterly resentful. It had taken weeks of quiet listening, observing, and coaxing from the women who heard things in the factory and the streets, but Katherine had finally begun to piece it together.

Now she would use it.

If she could prove who Marcus truly was—and what he had become—she might finally hold a weapon sharp enough to cut herself free.

And so she wrote.

A letter, penned slowly by firelight that evening, addressed not to Marcus, nor to any official, but to Lord Montclair himself. She wrote not as a blackmailer, but as a witness. She described what she had seen: the corrupt dealings, the coercion, the false deliveries. She made no demands, only laid bare what might soon be made public if Montclair did not act.

She signed only with her initials and a promise: *I know who he is. And what he's done. If you value silence, you will listen.*

She folded it carefully and placed it within an envelope, which she pressed into the hands of a stable-boy near the Montclair estate the following day.

"Give it only to the butler," she told him. "No one else." She slipped him a coin—more than she could spare—and prayed it would reach the right eyes.

HENRY CALLED THE NEXT EVENING, bringing with him a new tonic for Nora and a small loaf he claimed was a gift from a grateful patient. His kindness had not waned, but Katherine saw how his worry deepened. He watched her more closely now, his questions more pointed.

"I saw a bruised woman at the infirmary today," he said, as he sat by the fire. "Her husband had struck her. She wouldn't name him. She said she didn't want trouble."

Katherine looked up. "It's always trouble, isn't it? Whether you speak or stay silent."

Henry nodded. "But silence doesn't save you. It just delays the storm."

She reached for the mug of tea he'd made for her. "Do you think I've made a mistake?"

"I think you've done what you had to. But if you're planning something now, I want to help."

"I know," she said quietly. "And I may ask for it soon."

He didn't press. He only touched her hand gently, the warmth of it lingering long after he left.

MEANWHILE, Marcus Denton grew restless.

He arrived at the factory unannounced two days later, pacing the outer office like a man with a stone in his shoe. The foreman watched him with unease; the girls with open fear. When Katherine stepped into view, Marcus's gaze snapped to her.

"We need to speak," he said under his breath.

She nodded and followed him out.

He led her to a narrow alley just beyond the factory gates, where the scent of coal smoke and rotting fish clung to the walls.

"I've heard a rumour," he said. "That you've been sneaking around where you shouldn't"

Katherine kept her expression still. "I don't know what you mean."

He stepped closer, his voice low. "Don't play coy. I have eyes everywhere"

She lifted her chin. "You'd threaten a woman who's done everything you've asked? A mother whose only crime was trying to keep her child alive?"

Marcus's eyes narrowed. "You think I won't? I built this from nothing, Katherine. I won't let anyone tear it down—least of all someone like you."

She met his gaze evenly. "And yet, I don't think your real name would sound so good in the papers. Or in Montclair's drawing room."

His face went slack. Just for a second. But it was enough.

"You don't know what you're talking about."

"Oh, I think I do. And I think *he* would be very interested in knowing how you've used that name to open doors—and close others permanently."

His breath came faster now, and for the first

time, Katherine saw fear flash in his eyes. Then it vanished, replaced with a grin that didn't reach his eyes.

"You've got nerve," he said softly. "But nerve won't save you."

Katherine turned without replying. But her hands shook as she walked away.

She knew then: Marcus wouldn't wait. He would strike soon.

THAT NIGHT, she made her way to Ned Riley's quarters.

She'd heard that he'd been released from police custody and while she was quite sure that he didn't think that his arrest had anything to do with her, she could still feel the nerves start to overwhelm her.

But desperate times called for desperate measures, and this was a desperate thing, seeking out the man who had once terrified her, whose name still made her skin crawl.

But Ned, for all his violence, hated Marcus Denton almost as much as she did.

He opened the door with suspicion, a bottle in one hand, the stench of gin thick in the air.

"Katherine" he said. "Didn't think I'd see you again. You here to grovel? Or to warn?"

"Neither," she said, stepping inside. "I have an offer."

Ned laughed. "You offering anything is a surprise."

"I want Denton gone. You do too."

"And?"

"I'll tell you where he keeps the books. His ledgers. Names. Addresses. You can burn him with those. But I want your word—when he falls, I walk away clean. My name stays out of it."

Ned tilted his head. "And you trust me?"

"No," she said. "But I trust that you hate Marcus more than you hate me."

He considered her, then spat on the floor.

"You've changed," he said. "I used to scare you."

"You still do," she replied. "But not as much as he does."

He nodded slowly. "Deal."

But she lied.

Katherine had no intention of letting Ned Riley take the fall for her. He was a brute. If she fed him false information—enough to keep him busy—she could use the distraction to make her real move.

. . .

THAT MOVE CAME the next morning.

While Ned stormed through the dockside trying to shake down Marcus's men, Katherine returned to the old tailor's shop where she had once made deliveries.

Beneath the floorboards, where Marcus had hidden his ledgers wrapped in oilcloth, she retrieved the real prize. Dates. Codes. Names. Payments. And Montclair's.

She copied every word.

By evening, Henry had the list. She told him everything—her conversation with Marcus, her meeting with Ned, her fear.

He didn't flinch.

"I think we have enough," he said. "If we can get this to my friend the magistrate, then I think this, with everything else we've already given him can be used to open a case. Denton's connections won't matter if the press catch hold of this. Especially not with Montclair's name tied to it."

"Do it," she said.

He took her hand. "But are you sure?"

"Yes," she said. "I'm done being afraid."

THE NEXT NIGHT, Marcus Denton vanished.

No one saw him at the factory. His usual haunts were silent.

Even Ned Riley, when he came raging back to the boarding house with two blackened eyes and no ledgers, muttered, "He's gone. Slipped away like smoke."

But an article was published two days later. A quiet column in a small paper, naming no names— but detailing corruption, bribery, smuggling. The story grew by the hour. And soon, Marcus's face would be everywhere.

Katherine sat at the window, Nora asleep in her lap, and watched the world turn.

She had survived.

But more than that, she had *fought*.

CHAPTER 16

The room was quiet save for the soft crackle of the fire. Katherine sat by the hearth, her hands wrapped around a steaming mug, the scent of chamomile rising with the smoke. Across from her, Henry leaned against the worn sill of the window, watching the snow begin to fall. The silence between them was not uneasy; it was weighted with things unsaid, yet known.

"She's getting better," Henry said at last, his voice gentle. "Nora's colour is stronger. And Liam's spirits seem higher."

Katherine nodded, her eyes on the flames. "Because of you. Because you cared enough to help when no one else would."

Henry crossed the room, kneeling before her.

"No. Because you fought for them. You've done everything you could, even when the world offered nothing in return."

She looked at him then, eyes shining. "And I would do it again. I will do whatever I must. But I don't want to do it alone anymore."

He reached for her hand, lacing his fingers through hers. "Then don't. Katherine, I love you. I have for some time now. I didn't know how to say it... didn't want to presume."

A tear slid down her cheek, and she smiled, brushing it away. "I love you too, Henry. I think I did from the moment you placed your hand on Nora's forehead and didn't flinch."

They leaned in, foreheads touching, and for a moment the world outside ceased to exist. It was only them, only the warmth of shared trust and quiet certainty.

Katherine drew back slightly, her expression turning serious. "Then you deserve to know every-thing. Not just the pieces I've let slip."

She told him. About Marcus Denton. About the deliveries. About the money and the threat. About the constables in Denton's pocket and the web tightening around her. About Ned and her past. About the reason that she left Ireland and made her way to England with only herself and her children.

Henry listened, his face still, his hand never leaving hers.

"They have people everywhere," she said. "If I vanish, they'll know. If I stay, I'm a pawn. And my children..."

Henry stood, pacing. "You're not staying. Not like this. We'll find a way. But I need time."

"I've kept notes," Katherine admitted. "Letters he's sent. Slips with addresses. I never trusted him entirely."

Henry's mouth quirked, something like admiration in his eyes. "Good. We'll use them. But first, we need to get the children safe."

Together, they crafted a plan. A vicar Henry trusted had a cottage in the countryside, long disused but still intact. He would take Nora and Liam there himself within the week, once preparations were made. No one would think to look for them there.

Katherine resisted at first. "I should go too."

But Henry shook his head. "You're the one Denton watches. If you disappear with them, he'll know. If I go alone, they're merely children sent to a relative."

Reluctantly, she agreed. The plan was painful but sound. Meanwhile, Henry would reach out to his uncle—a barrister with enough influence to start inquiries that didn't lead back to them. They would gather evidence quietly, and when the moment came, strike decisively.

In the days that followed, Katherine worked as usual, keeping her head down. While Marcus may have disappeared she knew that he wouldn't be far. He would be keeping a close eye on her.

Of that she was certain. And not only that but what whatever charges had been brought against Ned still seemed to be in question, meaning that he was also still a possible danger to her and the children.

Henry moved with swift precision. By the third day, the safehouse was ready. Supplies were stocked. The vicar had been told only that Henry was escorting the children of a widow in need. The truth, he said, would only place the man in danger.

On the morning they left, Katherine wrapped Nora in an extra shawl and kissed Liam's brow three times. She pressed into Henry's hands a small pouch with the last of her saved coins.

"You'll need them more than I," she said.

He didn't argue. He only looked at her, long and hard, as if trying to memorise every detail.

"When this is over," he whispered, "we begin again. You, me, and them. Somewhere no one knows our names."

She nodded, unable to speak.

When they were gone, their room felt hollow. Katherine folded their blankets, cleaned the small table, swept the hearth. She could not sit still. She could not weep. There was no room now for anything but resolve.

That night, as the wind howled down the chimney and shadows crept across the walls, Katherine unwrapped the old tin box hidden beneath a floorboard. Inside were the notes, slips of paper, and coin ledgers Denton had once given her. She arranged them by date, copied the most important information, and sealed it all in a clean envelope.

Now came the waiting.

But Katherine was no longer afraid. Her children were safe. Her heart was spoken for. And the man who had once used her desperation as a leash would soon learn what it meant to cross a woman with nothing left to lose but everything worth fighting for.

CHAPTER 17

⌘

*T*he knock came just after dusk—sharp, impatient, familiar.

Katherine had known he'd come. Still, the sound sent a jolt through her chest.

She opened the door with deliberate calm. Ned Riley stood there, shoulders hunched in his thick coat, eyes gleaming with fury beneath the brim of his cap.

"Don't make me wait, girl."

She stepped aside, let him pass into the room where only the embers of the fire lit the space. The children were gone—safe.

"I've no news," Katherine said before he could speak. "Not yet."

His mouth twisted. "Not good enough."

She barely saw the blow before it landed—his hand striking her cheekbone, sharp and sudden. She staggered back, one hand catching the table.

"You think this is a game?" he hissed. "I let you run once. Should've buried you then."

Blood welled on her lip. She tasted iron and fear.

"I need more time," she said, steadying her voice.

"You're out of time." He grabbed her wrist, squeezing hard enough to bruise. "You want your brats breathing come morning, you bring me Denton's next move. Clear?"

She nodded, breath shallow.

"Say it."

"I understand," she whispered.

He shoved her back and left. The door slammed behind him.

For a long moment, Katherine didn't move. Then she turned to the washbasin, dabbing at the blood with a scrap of cloth, each motion brittle and precise.

She had known Ned's violence. But this... this was a reminder. Of what he was. Of what she faced.

And what she must do.

The following evening, Marcus set the trap.

She had known that he hadn't really left the city. She had known that he been watching her. Watching and waiting. It seemed that he couldn't quite let her go and she knew that it would only be a matter of time before he contacted her. And he didn't disappoint. A note was placed under the door of her room and when she read it a chill came over her.

He summoned her to a warehouse she didn't recognise, its iron locks thick and rusting, its windows like dark eyes watching the alley. She entered cautiously, clutching her shawl close against the rain.

He stood by a table, a package wrapped in wax cloth before him. Two men loitered in the shadows —unfamiliar. Not his usual runners.

"You're late," he said, his tone even.

"You said midnight."

He gestured to the parcel. "Take this to the docks. Slip it beneath the pier stairs. No contact. No deviation."

She reached for it, but his gaze held hers like a snare.

"There's something else."

She froze.

"Henry Ellsworth," he said softly. "You've been seeing him often."

"He treats my daughter."

His smile curved, cold. "He asks questions. Watches places he shouldn't. Are you telling him things, Katherine?"

"No."

He stepped closer. "Because if you are... if you're thinking of betrayal... this city has no shortage of dark corners where women disappear."

"I'm loyal," she said.

"Good," he said. "Then prove it."

The moment stretched. Then: "Go."

She took the parcel and left, her heart hammering. It was a test—she knew that. Not of her ability, but of her obedience. Of her silence.

And she would fail it. Willingly.

She didn't go to the docks.

Instead, she slipped through side streets, found Henry waiting where they had arranged—beneath the gaslight at the edge of the square, shadowed by the colonnade of the magistrate's building.

He said nothing, only held out his hands. She gave him the parcel. He placed it in a satchel, sealed it beneath his coat.

As far as Katherine was concerned this was the

last of the evidence that would ever be needed. Not only to bring Marcus Denton to justice but also Ned.

This was the end of it all and she felt the relief of it all course through her as she let out a deep sigh.

THE NEXT MORNING, whispers filled the factory. A constable had been seen near the docks. A fire had broken out near Ashton's. Someone said Denton had been taken. Another claimed he had vanished.

Katherine said nothing.

She moved with quiet purpose, hands steady at her station. Mary gave her a long look, but didn't speak. They shared only a nod—an understanding. The worst had passed. Or was passing.

Later that day, Henry arrived.

"The magistrate's office has issued warrants," he said. "Denton's network is collapsing."

"And Ned?"

"Gone. They'll keep him locked."

She exhaled. "It's not just me now, Henry. It never was. There are women who need the same way out. We have to help them."

He looked at her—not surprised, only certain. "We will."

. . .

THAT NIGHT, Katherine returned to the small desk beneath the window. She wrote with care.

Names. Facts. Routes. A ledger of her own, not for trade or coin—but for justice.

The danger hadn't ended. But neither had she.

She was no longer a smuggler.

No longer a ghost of survival.

She was a mother. A fighter. A witness.

And she would not be silent.

CHAPTER 18

The wind rattled the panes as Katherine sat hunched beside the hearth, the glow of the coals casting flickering shadows across her face. She held the folded letter between trembling fingers—a scrap of misleading information she had composed and delivered earlier that day.

It had taken every ounce of her nerve to write it, to mask the truth so artfully that Ned Riley would believe it. That the next shipment Marcus had arranged would pass through the south docks, late at night, unguarded. It was a lie, of course—the kind laced with enough truth to be believable. Ned wouldn't resist. Greed was his compass, and Katherine had steered it precisely where she needed.

She stared into the fire, feeling the weight of

what she'd done. She had started the double-cross. There would be no turning back now.

The knock came long after nightfall—sharp and urgent. She rose slowly, instinct coiling in her gut. When she opened the door, Marcus Denton stood there.

His coat was dusted with soot and rain. His expression—calm, calculated—didn't match the fury that simmered in his eyes.

"We need to talk," he said.

Before she could answer, he stepped inside. His hand closed around her arm, firm but not bruising— yet. The door clicked shut behind him. The room suddenly felt too small, too dim.

"You lied to me," he said, low and cold.

Katherine's mouth went dry. "I don't know what you mean."

His hand tightened. "Don't insult me."

He dragged her forward, her shawl slipping from her shoulders. She tried to wrench free, but he was too strong.

"You gave Riley information," Marcus hissed. "Do you think I wouldn't find out? That my people wouldn't see you drop that letter?"

She swallowed hard, her mind racing. "You were using me."

He laughed bitterly. "Of course I was. Just as you were using me."

He shoved her back against the wall, though not hard. His breathing was uneven now, and behind the anger, she saw something else—hurt.

"Why?" he asked, voice quieter. "Why betray me?"

The question caught her off guard. He wasn't demanding. He sounded genuinely... wounded.

"You said I was different," he muttered. "That I wasn't like them. I believed you."

Katherine blinked. "I never lied about that. But you gave me no choice, Marcus."

He let go of her, stepping back. His face twisted as though something inside him was breaking apart.

"I protected you," he said. "I kept the police from your door. I paid for that bloody medicine."

"You bought control," she snapped. "You used my daughter's suffering to tie my hands."

His jaw clenched. He turned away, as though the sight of her was too much.

And then, suddenly, he turned back, his voice trembling with fury. "You think I haven't suffered? That I haven't clawed my way through blood and ash to get where I am? Everything I built—everything I did—was because no one ever gave a damn about boys like me."

"You chose this," Katherine said. "You didn't have to drag others into it."

For a long, terrible moment, silence pressed between them. Then his hand darted forward, seizing her wrist.

"You don't get to walk away," he snarled.

But something had changed. His grip lacked its usual power. His movements, once so precise, were sloppy with emotion. Katherine's heart pounded. She twisted hard, breaking free—and ran.

The door slammed against the wall as she burst into the corridor. She could hear his boots behind her, pounding the floorboards, but he was a step too slow.

She flew down the stairs, skirts snagging at her ankles, feet skidding on the worn steps. At the landing, she stumbled. A hand closed on the back of her dress—but it was too late.

"Katherine!"

She heard her name shouted—but it wasn't Marcus's voice.

She looked up as Henry Ellsworth appeared in the boarding house doorway, his eyes wide with alarm. Without hesitation, he stepped forward, interposing himself between her and Marcus, whose momentum faltered.

"Get away from her," Henry said, voice low and calm—but with an edge that brooked no refusal.

Marcus froze. His eyes flicked between them, calculating.

"She's made a mistake," Marcus said smoothly. "She's in danger."

"I've seen the danger," Henry replied. "And I won't let you touch her again."

A flicker of something—fear? grief?—passed across Marcus's face. Then, with a sneer, he stepped back.

"You've no idea what you're doing, doctor. You think this ends with me walking away? It doesn't."

"I know exactly what I'm doing," Henry said. "Now go."

For a moment, it seemed Marcus might lunge again—but then he turned sharply, his coat sweeping behind him as he stormed out into the night.

Katherine collapsed against the bannister, her lungs burning. Henry was beside her in an instant, steadying her with gentle hands.

"I saw him go in," he said. "Something felt wrong."

She could hardly speak, her throat tight with shock. "I didn't expect—he was so angry... but not just that. He looked—lost."

Henry guided her to a chair, kneeling before her.

"What did you do?" he asked gently.

Katherine stared at him. And then she told him everything. About the letter. About the fake shipment. About Ned Riley. About her plan to pit the wolves against one another.

Henry listened without interruption, his expression unreadable.

"You're trying to bring them down," he said at last.

She nodded.

"It's dangerous," he said. "But it might work."

She blinked. "You don't think I'm mad?"

"I think you're desperate," he said. "But brave. And clever."

A silence settled between them, heavy and fragile. Then he took her hand.

"I'll help you."

Katherine's eyes filled, but she blinked the tears away.

"There's more," she said. "Riley won't hesitate. If Marcus shows up where I told him to be..."

"There'll be blood," Henry finished grimly.

"Yes."

CHAPTER 19

*he morning of the exhibition dawned grey and mist-laden, the spires of the Crystal Palace rising like the bones of some ancient creature through the fog. Katherine's breath caught as she approached the gates, her heart pounding in rhythm with the polished boots that clattered on the surrounding cobblestones. Henry's words echoed in her ears: *Be careful. And trust no one but yourself.*

This was it.

The plan had been carefully constructed over weeks, stitched together with quiet meetings, false trails, and the risky alliance with Henry and the magistrate. Today, with thousands streaming toward the Palace to see the marvels of industry and invention, Marcus Denton would be exposed for what he truly was—and Ned Riley, too, if all went according to plan.

Katherine moved with the crowd.

Inside, the hall glittered with glass and steel. Banners unfurled from high arches, displays of machinery, exotic goods, and elaborate scientific curiosities filled the space. And at the far end—at the back of it all—was Marcus's private display. Smuggled antiquities. Illicit gems. All masked beneath the guise of colonial marvels.

Henry appeared at her side. She hadn't seen him approach, but she knew the tight line of his jaw, the way his eyes scanned the crowd.

"They're all in place," he said quietly. "The magistrate's men are circling the perimeter. Riley's in the western wing. Denton arrived fifteen minutes ago."

Katherine nodded once. Her hands trembled, but she forced herself still. "Then it begins."

It began with a commotion.

Two constables—real ones—moved toward Marcus's display, asking questions. Not loud enough to alarm the crowd, but firm. Intentional. The kind of questions that could not be brushed off. Marcus, ever composed, welcomed them with false charm. His eyes flicked up, searching. He hadn't seen Katherine yet.

But Ned Riley had.

He stood near one of the central columns, watching her. His thick frame wove through the crowd, his expression thunderous. Katherine felt it like a change in the wind. She turned sharply, ushering the children toward a quieter section.

Too late.

Riley caught her arm, spinning her around. "You think you can double-cross me?" he snarled, loud enough that people turned. "You Irish whore—"

A constable intervened—but not one of Henry's. This one Katherine recognised from the alley near the boarding house. One of Marcus's.

Katherine's blood chilled.

Then chaos erupted.

Someone shouted. A woman screamed. A gunshot cracked through the glass dome overhead, and the crowd surged like a wave.

Another shot. This time from Henry.

She saw Riley stagger, saw the red bloom on his shirt. Then he lunged—toward Henry, toward her, it wasn't clear—but a second shot felled him. He collapsed onto the floor, his eyes wide with shock. His last breath rattled out between his teeth.

Marcus, in the distance, tried to flee.

But Katherine wasn't the only one with a plan.

The magistrate's men descended. They had waited until they had enough—until Denton's dealings were not merely suspected but proven, until his attempt to escape was itself a confession.

He was seized at the steps beneath the eastern gallery.

Someone called out his name—not Marcus Denton, but *Montclair*. Lord Montclair's bastard son. A scandal long buried, now unearthed in front of hundreds.

HOURS PASSED. Statements were taken. Marcus was carted off in chains, his face still trying to arrange itself into civility. He failed. Henry found them just before dusk, his coat torn, a bruise forming beneath one eye.

"It's done," he said simply.

They returned to the boarding house in silence. Mary met them at the door, eyes wide, hands trembling.

That night, Katherine sat by the fire.

Henry sat across from her, nursing tea.

"You saved more than just yourself," he said. "You gave them the evidence they needed. Marcus, Riley —the corruption in the force. All of it."

She stared into the flames. "At what cost?"

He didn't answer.

She didn't expect him to.

Because even though she was safe now—even though the danger had passed—the price of survival was steep.

The children were changed. She was changed.

And though the city outside carried on, oblivious to all she had endured, Katherine knew the ghosts of that day would follow her for years to come.

Still, as the fire crackled and Henry's steady presence anchored her, a small ember of peace began to glow.

They had survived.

It wasn't victory.

But it was enough to begin again.

CHAPTER 20

*orning came grey and damp, and with it, Henry.

He knocked quietly, as he always did, and entered only when she called out. He brought bread and smoked fish, a fresh poultice for Nora's chest, and a flask of something hot and herbal that steamed between them.

Katherine didn't rise to greet him. She couldn't yet muster the shape of kindness. But her eyes softened at the sight of him, and when he set the food down and took the seat opposite her, she didn't look away.

He poured a measure of tea into a chipped mug and offered it without a word.

"Thank you," she said, her voice low.

They sat in silence for a time, the clock ticking on the mantel, the street sounds bleeding faintly through the glass.

Finally, Henry said, "I saw Billingham yesterday. Marcus Denton has been moved to Newgate."

Katherine didn't speak.

"They've charged him with conspiracy, fraud, bribery of public officials. It may take weeks to sort it all—but the case is strong."

Still, she said nothing.

"He asked for you," Henry added, more gently. "Said he wanted to speak. One last time."

Her eyes lifted at last, wary and tired. "Why?"

"I don't know."

A pause stretched between them, heavy with all the things unsaid.

"Will you go?" he asked.

"I don't know," she whispered.

Henry nodded and didn't press further. His patience was a balm she hadn't known she needed. In another man, it would have been pressure disguised as sympathy. In him, it was space—given freely.

He stood, slowly. "I'll come back this evening, if you want me to."

Katherine met his gaze. "You can stay now. If you like."

He hesitated, then returned to the chair and folded his hands in his lap.

Together, they watched the fire struggle back to life.

It was Mary who coaxed her out later that day, wrapping her arm firmly through Katherine's and insisting they walk to the market.

"Fresh air," she said. "And a bit of normal."

They passed the butcher's stall, the baker with the ginger curls, the familiar soot-caked windows of the apothecary where Henry sometimes fetched supplies.

To Katherine's surprise, people greeted her.

A nod here, a murmured *'Glad you're safe'* there. Not effusive. Not insistent. But real.

Even the grocer's wife, who once scowled when Liam so much as touched the apple barrels, pressed a small paper bag of sugared almonds into Katherine's hand.

"For the little one," she said gruffly.

Mary caught Katherine's startled glance and gave

her arm a squeeze. "They know what you did. Word spreads, love. Especially when it's the truth."

They returned home with potatoes and a fresh loaf, and though Katherine said little, something inside her eased. Just slightly.

THAT NIGHT, with the children back eith her in the room at the lodging house and fast asleep, the lamps burning low, Henry read from one of the borrowed books he brought each week.

A tale of swallows and far-off cliffs, of letters carried across the sea. His voice was steady, his tone warm.

Katherine sat nearby, sewing a patch into Nora's nightdress.

When the story ended, silence fell again. Henry closed the book and leaned back.

"You've been quieter," he said gently.

She set her sewing aside. "I keep thinking it's over—but it never really is, is it?"

"No," he said. "But the worst is past."

She met his eyes. "Is it?"

He studied her. "Do you still feel hunted?"

"Not hunted. Just... hollow. Like I've buried

something too deep, and now I don't know how to dig it back up."

Henry leaned forward. "You don't have to rush. Healing's not a straight road. And you've been walking broken ground for a long time."

She didn't speak. But when he reached across and took her hand, she didn't pull away.

Days passed. Then a letter came, delivered by a boy who wouldn't meet her eyes.

It was short. Barely a sentence.

Please. Just once. – M.

Katherine read it three times before setting it on the fire. But she didn't burn it.

Not yet.

She found herself at Newgate three days later.

Henry had said nothing when she told him she was going. Just nodded and offered to wait nearby.

Inside, the air was thick with rot and rust. A gaoler led her down a narrow corridor, the sound of keys and boots echoing like gunfire in a cathedral.

Marcus sat behind the bars. His coat was gone,

his hair unkempt. But he still managed to look composed, even elegant.

"Katherine," he said softly.

She stood with her hands folded, chin high.

"I didn't expect you to come."

"I wasn't sure I would."

He nodded, as though that made sense. "I wanted to say—I'm sorry."

She frowned. "For what? The lies? The threats? The way you used my child as leverage?"

His gaze dropped. "All of it."

She waited. No protest. No justification. Just silence.

"I believed I was saving you," he said at last. "From worse men. From poverty. I thought... if I kept you close, you'd be safe."

"You never made me feel safe."

"I know."

Katherine swallowed. "Why now, Marcus? Why this?"

"Because I've lost," he said. "And you haven't."

Something in her flinched.

"You still have them—your children. Your dignity. You have someone who looks at you with... real eyes." His voice cracked slightly. "I never had that."

Katherine stared at him, stunned by the honesty. "You had choices."

He nodded. "And I made the wrong ones."

They stood in silence again. The air between them was no longer angry—just old. Like dust on an unopened book.

"Tell Nora I'm glad she's well," he said. "And tell her... I'm sorry I ever made her mother cry."

It was all the apology he had to give.

She left without another word.

THE SEASON TURNED. Cold mornings softened into warmer ones. The smoke from the chimneys still blackened the sky, but now it mingled with birdsong.

Nora was walking again—steadily now—and helping Mary peel vegetables in the kitchen. Liam played in the yard with pegs and sticks, his laughter echoing off the alley walls.

And Katherine stood at the window, watching them, a blanket wrapped tight around her shoulders.

Henry came in quietly, carrying a tin of tea.

"They're blooming," he said, nodding toward the children.

She smiled faintly. "They are."

He poured her a cup and offered it, his fingers brushing hers.

"I still don't know if I'll ever feel... whole," she admitted.

"You might not," he said gently. "But you're alive. And you're healing. That's enough to begin."

They stood together, watching the morning light dance on the wall.

And for the first time in a long time, Katherine didn't feel like she was drowning.

She wasn't quite free. Not yet.

But she was no longer trapped.

And that, for now, was enough.

Chapter Twenty One

Katherine stood at the threshold of the narrow doorway, the key cold and foreign in her palm. She turned it slowly in the lock, her heart thudding, and pushed open the door to the first home she could call her own since leaving Ireland.

It wasn't much—two rooms stacked one above the other, with a narrow stair and a cracked window that looked out over a courtyard lined with drying linen. But it was hers. The landlord, an elderly man with rheumy eyes, had taken her payment without question, and for the first time in years, she had a roof secured by her own hand, not the charity or danger of others.

Nora stepped hesitantly inside, her small feet leaving faint marks on the dusty floorboards. Liam followed, wide-eyed.

"It's warm," he said softly.

Warm might have been generous, but there was a hearth, and Mary had sent them off with a kettle and two heavy blankets.

Mary, who was now more family than a friend and as such had come with them to this new home.

Katherine dropped the bag of their belongings onto the table and turned, taking it in—each cracked tile, each beam of warped wood—as if memorising the exact dimensions of her newfound safety.

This was the beginning.

Nora crossed to the hearth and knelt, placing her hand against the bricks. Her cheeks, still pale from illness, had gained the faintest blush of returning health, and Katherine's throat tightened.

"We'll have a fire in here tonight," Katherine said. "And I'll make us bread with what's left of the flour. Tomorrow, I'll find more."

Nora turned, smiling. "Can we put up my drawing? The one Mary gave me?"

"We'll hang it above your bed," Katherine replied, smiling as Liam ran his fingers along the wooden table with childlike reverence.

Outside, the street noise murmured on—carts rolling, voices lifting, the occasional call of a coster-monger—but in here, there was stillness. Safety. Katherine let herself feel it.

They were home.

Two days passed in a kind of domestic rhythm that Katherine had thought lost to her forever. Henry visited, bringing apples and a new pair of shoes for Liam, pretending they were a gift from an old patient of his.

Katherine saw through it but said nothing. Nora, now strong enough to climb the stairs alone, had even helped Katherine sweep the hearth and arrange their small pile of belongings.

It was on the third morning, after Liam had gone with Mary to fetch milk, that Henry asked to speak to her alone.

He stood near the fire, holding his hat in both hands.

"Katherine," he began, "I've been meaning to say

something, but I didn't wish to press you while Nora was unwell."

She looked up from where she knelt, tying a bundle of kindling. "Go on."

His voice softened. "I would like to marry you."

She froze.

He continued before she could speak. "Not because of charity. Not out of obligation. I've seen your strength, your devotion to your children, your cleverness and your courage." He stepped forward. "You are unlike anyone I have known."

Katherine stared at him. A thousand thoughts surged in her mind—of Marcus, of secrets she had not yet dared share, of the risks that still haunted her. And yet, there was Henry—his steady presence, his gentle patience. He had asked nothing of her but her honesty, and offered all the warmth and safety she'd long thought reserved for others.

"You deserve a better woman than me," she said, voice low.

"I'm not looking for better," he replied, "only for you."

She let out a shaky breath, one hand braced against the floor. "Let me think on it."

"Of course," he said, and bowed his head before taking his leave.

But the question lingered like smoke in the air long after he was gone.

LATER, as she walked the riverbank toward home, the city's cold wind biting at her cheeks, Katherine felt the ache of long-held tension begin to ease.

Back at the house, Nora met her at the door.

"Henry came by," she said. "He left this."

She held out a small wrapped bundle. Inside, Katherine found a tin of salve for her hands and a note: *"For the woman who builds futures."* It was signed simply, *H*.

That evening, Katherine tucked Liam and Nora into bed and sat by the hearth, staring into the fire.

Then she rose, walked to the table, and took out a clean sheet of paper.

Henry, she wrote, *I would be honoured.*

THE END

Printed in Dunstable, United Kingdom